Plastic Indian

D0746522

AMERICAN INDIAN LITERATURE AND CRITICAL STUDIES SERIES

Robert J. Conley, 2008.
Photograph by Mark Haskett, Western Carolina University.

Plastic Indian

A COLLECTION OF STORIES
AND OTHER WRITINGS

∼ ∼ ∼

Robert J. Conley

Edited by Evelyn L. Conley
Foreword by Geary Hobson

UNIVERSITY OF OKLAHOMA PRESS : NORMAN

Publication of this book is made possible through the generosity of Edith Kinney Gaylord.

"Plastic Indian" was previously published in the following anthologies and journal: George Brose and Kate Egerton, eds., *Appalachian Gateway: An Anthology of Contemporary Stories and Poetry* (Knoxville: University of Tennessee Press, 2013); Christopher Murphy, ed., *Green Country: Writing from Northeast Oklahoma* (Tahlequah, Okla.: Save the Illinois River, 2016); and *Appalachian Heritage* 37, no. 4 (Fall 2009).

"How Robert Whitekiller Got a New Name and Found His Own Grave" was previously published in *Appalachian Heritage* 37, no. 2 (Spring 2009).

"A Reevaluation of Sequoyah's Final Trip" was previously published in the *Journal of Cherokee Studies* 27 (2009).

Plastic Indian: A Collection of Stories and Other Writings is Volume 71 in the American Indian Literature and Critical Studies Series.

Library of Congress Cataloging-in-Publication Data

Names: Conley, Robert J., author. | Conley, Evelyn L., 1949– editor. |
 Hobson, Geary, writer of foreword.
Title: Plastic Indian : a collection of stories and other writings / Robert J. Conley ;
 edited by Evelyn L. Conley ; foreword by Geary Hobson.
Description: Norman : University of Oklahoma Press, 2018. | Series: American
 Indian literature and critical studies ; Volume 71
Identifiers: LCCN 2018002452 | ISBN 978-0-8061-6151-8 (pbk. : alk. paper)
Classification: LCC PS3553.O494 A6 2018 | DDC 818/.5409—dc23
LC record available at https://lccn.loc.gov/2018002452

The paper in this book meets the guidelines for permanence and durability of the Committee on Production Guidelines for Book Longevity of the Council on Library Resources, Inc. ∞

～) (～) (～)

*To all Cherokees, everywhere, who believe
we have a great literary history to live up to,
to move into, and to be a part of.*

*This work is a part of that history,
and the stories yet to be written are endless.*

Contents

Foreword

GEARY HOBSON

I first met Robert J. Conley in the mid-1970s through the small press exchange that was the writer's internet back then. We corresponded for a while (by letter, not email), until finally one day in the summer of 1977, we met in person, and I spent an afternoon with him in his home near Hulbert, Oklahoma. This was before he began writing and publishing the remarkable westerns for which he has become famous, although, as I recall, he was already at the time well on his way toward that goal. I was delighted to learn that, just as had been true for me, as a teenager he had discovered and valued such magazines as *True West, Frontier Times*, and *True Western Adventures*. We both had delighted in reading and discovering the real West, as best we could—including people such as the real Billy the Kid and John Wesley Hardin, and the real Wyatt Earp, who was a much more unsavory type than the sanitized Hugh O'Brian depiction of him on TV—through our out-of-school reading. Bob's real strength as a writer of western fiction is grounded in this realism, and his work is nothing like the so-called shoot-'em-ups that tend to stand as the definition of the genre. As well, it is doubtful that there are many other writers whose portrayal of western lawmen and outlaws is as strongly grounded in such realism. And, too, his depiction of Cherokee culture and history, particularly of the last half of the nineteenth century, remains just about the best you'll find among all the writers who have deigned to write about Cherokee life and culture and history.

Although he is revered for his novels, the present volume—a posthumous collection of short stories, essays, public addresses, and a small play—demonstrates ample evidence of his abilities in other genres. The short stories often display the same sort of grim realism that characterizes his novels—with the exception of the title story, "Plastic Indian." This one is sheer comedy, reminiscent of the short fiction collections of Ring Lardner and A. B. Guthrie Jr., and is set in contemporary times. "Brass," the short radio play, is a retelling of one of the numerous traditional Cherokee folktales that are amply featured in James Mooney's classic anthropological work *Myths of the Cherokee* (1900).

With Robert J. Conley's passing in 2014, contemporary Native American literature—and Oklahoma and U.S. literatures as well—lost a unique and major figure. May his work continue to delight and instruct all of us who are fortunate enough to read it.

Editor's Preface

EVELYN L. CONLEY

This group of stories and other writings by Robert J. Conley was waiting in a folder for the right time to be published. Thanks to an inquisitive editor at the University of Oklahoma Press who knew these pieces existed and had worked with the author in the past on any number of books that were published by OU Press, this collection is now being made available for all to enjoy.

Robert J. Conley's last speech and public reading was given at the Eighth Annual Jan Wyatt Symposium, held at the High Hampton Inn in Cashiers, North Carolina, on Thursday, May 23, 2013. The topic of his presentation was "What It Means to Be Cherokee." Serving as the Sequoyah Distinguished Professor of Cherokee Studies at Western Carolina University, Conley was often asked to participate in and provide keynote information on Cherokee history and culture to any number of groups. This collection opens with his speech from that day, which was followed by a reading of "Plastic Indian."

In this collection of writings, Conley provides insight into the lives of Cherokees, detailing experiences that allow us to observe the kinds of everyday situations that have been part of the ongoing journey of what it means to be Cherokee. He captures the thoughts, feelings, and actions that define how we determine who we are and why we should believe in who we are. In addition to the stories, a short radio play, adapted from the writings of James Mooney, gives us a look into historic Cherokee lore. Conley was an avid fan of the western cowboy story and couldn't resist writing a couple of stories in that genre, as you will discover in "The Execution" and "Nate's Revenge." Finally, this collection ends with four speeches that he purposely selected for inclusion and felt were significant milestones. A very special thanks to Jan D. Hodge, who helped to edit the manuscript for publication and reworked "Aunt Jenny" from Conley's notes and rough draft.

Robert J. Conley, my husband, passed from this life on February 16, 2014.

Plastic Indian

What It Means to Be Cherokee

So what does it mean to be Cherokee? I'm just one man, so I can't answer that for all Cherokees, or for any Cherokee other than myself. But for me, it means—first of all—knowing where you came from, knowing the people you came from. I know all about my father and his mother and her father and grandfather and on back until the time of George Washington. I know they were Cherokees.

And it means knowing what they went through—knowing our history. It means knowing that Cherokees fought with the British during the American Revolution. I have ancestors who fought on that British side, and I know and understand why they did that.

It means knowing about the Trail of Tears and why it happened. And it means knowing Oklahoma and how Oklahoma land became Cherokee land. Most of my life, the only Cherokee land I knew was Oklahoma, but I knew about the Cherokee land out here from reading. I knew that this was the land they kicked us off when they sent us west to what became Oklahoma.

Finally I got to come out here, to Cullowhee and to Cherokee, and I felt at home right away. That's something else that being Cherokee means. It means that no matter where one was born, when one comes to this part of the country, to Cherokee or any of the surrounding area, one feels immediately at home, for this was all Cherokee land. And that is the first thing that being Cherokee means to me.

Then it means feeling a part of a Cherokee community. And that means feeling some responsibility for that community—feeling that it has given you something of worth, and feeling that you have to give something back.

It means listening to the Cherokee storytellers, because their stories not only are entertaining, they are also teaching stories. They teach us what it means to be Cherokee, what we have to know and how we have to behave. Cherokee beliefs are based in faith in what the elders taught, and our contemporary storytellers learned their stories from their elders. So now they are telling us those stories. If we are really Cherokee, we need to listen to those stories. We need to learn, and we need to do our best to live by what we have learned from them.

We can't ignore our ancient roots, but we have to live modern. We have to be able to take care of ourselves and our families. That usually means having a job and doing it well. We have to make enough money to pay our bills, to buy food and clothes. Whatever we need, we have to work for it.

We have to respect women—all women. Women brought us into the world, and women keep us going. And we have to love children, for the children will keep the people going. One day they will be the people, and if we want our culture to survive, we have to respect our children and bring them up in the right way. Bring them up to have respect for all things.

If you see someone who is hungry, feed him. Take care of your neighbors. That's what we're here for—to take care of each other. Remember that laughter is perhaps the best medicine there is. So try to always have a good sense of humor.

I write stories. I write books. And mostly when I write, I write it because I feel like it is not well enough known, and I want people to know about it. For example, I remember that when I was going to school, there was a little box (they call it a sidebar) in our history book about the Trail of Tears. It was like a footnote, and that's all there was. And that's all that most people know about Cherokees. So I wrote a novel about the Trail of Tears, and I called it *Mountain Windsong*. I'm happy to say that it has been widely read. It has been used in high school and college classes around the country. So at least some people know more about the Trail of Tears now than they did before I wrote that book. It's still being used today. I recently received an email from a teacher in a school somewhere way up north telling me how much her students are enjoying that book. They're learning, too.

I don't write only about history. I write some stories that are contemporary, and I'm going to read one to you now. This one is being turned into a movie—I hope real soon. It's called "Plastic Indian," and it's about some Cherokees I knew in Oklahoma and what some of their concerns were.

CHEROKEE TALES

Plastic Indian

～

We had driven past it dozens, perhaps hundreds, of times, the giant plastic Indian that stood in front of the motel on Highway 51, and we had almost always cussed it as we went by. It was an insult to us all. One feather in its hair, a pair of moccasins, and a flap on its front and back were all the clothes it wore. It stood with one leg straight and the other slightly bent at the knee as it held one hand up against its head for an eye shade. Its hair was long and worn in two braids, which dangled on its chest. Perhaps worst of all, its flesh was pink. It stood there, towering over us as we drove from Tahlequah to Tulsa or to any number of smaller towns along the way.

We came to view the big pink plastic Indian as a symbol of all that was wrong and all that was evil in our midst. Before 1907, the spot on which the plastic Indian stood had been definitely and unquestionably Cherokee. It had been part of the Cherokee Nation, a portion of the land that was owned by all Cherokees. But Oklahoma statehood had changed all of that. Before 1907, the Cherokee Nation had produced more college graduates than the states of Arkansas and Texas combined. By 1970, according to the U.S. census, the average adult Cherokee had but four and one-half years of school. Even Will Rogers had said, "We had the greatest territory in the world, and they ruined it when they made a state," or words to that effect. We all agreed with him, and we all further agreed that the plastic Indian was a symbol of all of that.

We had all been out drinking one summer's evening, and we were headed back toward Tahlequah when we drove past the plastic Indian.

"Look at that ugly son of a bitch," Tom said.

"We've been looking at it for years," said Pat.

"We talk about it every time we drive past here," I said.

"We've talked long enough," said Tom. "Let's do something about it."

"Like what?"

"Let's tear the damn thing down once and for all."

The plastic Indian was already well behind us and long out of sight, but the conversation continued. Perhaps it was all the beer we had consumed. Perhaps the timing was just right. Who knows? But the talk just kept going. It wouldn't stop.

"How are we going to do that?" I asked.

"Drive out to my house," Tom said, "and I'll show you."

By the time we got to Tom's house in the Rocky Ford community on the other side of Tahlequah, Tom had passed out. None of us had any idea what he'd had in mind, so we rolled him out into his front yard and drove off. Nothing was done about the plastic Indian.

It was several days before we all got together again. We were at my house drinking beer, and for some reason, Tom started talking about the plastic Indian again. I don't recall our ever having talked about it before except when we had just driven past it. It was still early in the evening, too. I suspected that something might develop.

"That damn thing," Tom said, "is an insult to all of us. It would be bad enough if a white man put up a tall Indian that really looked like a Cherokee to advertise his business. But that thing doesn't even look like us. If anything, it looks like Longfellow's Hiawatha, or maybe Uncas from *The Last of the Mohicans*."

"It is an ugly bastard," I said, not being possessed of Tom's eloquence. I sipped some more beer from the wet can.

"Those guys think they can do anything right here in our own country," said Pat. "They're surrounded by Indians all the time. Hell, some of their customers are Indians."

"Most of them," said Tom.

"There's the U-Need-Um Tires company," I said, "and the U-Totem stores."

"That damn plastic Indian covers it all," said Tom. "Let's go."

Without waiting for an answer, Tom got up and headed out the front door. Pat and I followed, giving one another puzzled looks. Tom had an old pickup parked outside in my driveway, and we piled in. Tom fired the thing up and backed out into the street.

"Where are we going?" Pat asked.

"You'll see," said Tom.

"We're going out to look at that plastic Indian?" I asked.

"Yeah," Tom said. "That's where we're going."

"What are we going to do?" asked Pat.

"You'll see."

We were lucky the cops weren't out that night, because Tom ran four red lights and drove about ten miles over the speed limit all the way out to where the plastic Indian stood guard over the motel on Highway 51. He pulled over on the shoulder and stopped just across the road from the monstrosity. We all sat there in silence staring at it for several minutes. Then Tom got out of the pickup.

"You drive it, Pat," he said.

Pat had been sitting in the middle of the seat, so he scooted over behind the wheel. "Okay," he said, "but where are you going?"

"I'll be in the back," Tom said. "Drive on down the road a ways. Then turn around and drive back, and when you come up on that plastic Indian, don't slow down."

"What are you going to do?"

"Just drive," said Tom. He climbed into the pickup bed, and Pat gunned the engine. There were no cars coming, so he moved out onto the road in a hurry and drove on down for maybe a mile. Then he made a U-turn, and as he did, I saw Tom fall over in the back of the truck. Pat kept driving, and Tom got back up to his feet. I twisted my head to watch him, and I saw him pick up a coiled rope and pay out a loop. Tom was a frustrated cowboy. He was always talking about chasing wild horses on government land.

Up ahead, the plastic Indian came back into view. Pat roared ahead. In the back of the truck, Tom swung a wide loop over his head. He looked magnificent standing in the back of the speeding pickup spinning that loop. We came closer, and Tom threw the loop. I watched, fascinated, as it arced its way up and over the plastic head, but the fascination turned to horror as I saw the loop tighten, the rope straighten, and Tom go flying out of the back of the pickup.

"Stop!" I yelled to Pat.

Pat hit the brakes. "What's wrong?"

"We've lost Tom," I said. "Hell, we might've killed him."

"Damn."

The old pickup came to a stop on the shoulder. Pat shifted into low and made a U-turn. He drove back toward the plastic Indian, and we could see Tom struggling to his feet. Pat pulled up beside him.

"Get in," he said.

I opened the door and moved to the middle of the seat to make room, and Tom slid in with a moan.

"God damn," he said.

"What the hell were you trying to do?" Pat asked.

"I was going to rope that damn thing and pull it over," said Tom.

"Well, you roped it, all right," I said.

"Yeah."

Tom moaned again, and I asked, "Are you hurt?"

He lifted up his arms, and I could see that his shirt sleeves were in shreds, and even in the dark I could see where his arms had been skinned by the pavement.

"Jesus," I said. "You're lucky you're not dead."

When we got back to my house and in the light, we could see that not only Tom's arms, but also his chest and belly were skinned pretty bad. He was bleeding some. We washed him up and found some kind of salve to rub on the affected spots. His face had a couple of places on it, too, but they weren't too bad. To tell the truth, he had been remarkably lucky. If I had tried that fool trick, and if I'd been skillful enough to catch anything with the rope, I'd have been killed for sure.

"Son of a bitch," Tom said.

"What?"

"It's starting to hurt now."

It was a couple of weeks later when Pat and Tom drove up to my house in the old pickup again. They had a couple of six-packs with them. Actually, they had one six-pack and part of another. They had already broken into that one. I took one and opened it, drinking fast to catch up with them. We sat in my living room and drank and talked for a while. Then Pat said, "We got it figured out this time."

"What?" I said.

"We figured out how to pull down that plastic Indian."

"Bullshit," I said.

"No, really."

I looked at Tom. "He's right," he said. "We do have it figured out. You going to go out there with us?"

Well, I wouldn't have missed it for the world. We had to stop for some gas, but in a short while, we were on the way again.

"What's the plan?" I asked.

"It's brilliant," said Pat. "It's all Tom's idea."

"Well, what is it?"

"You'll see," said Tom.

"You're not going to sling something from the back of the truck again, are you?"

"No, nothing like that."

Tom still had scabs on parts of his body. As he drove through town, I kept wondering what grand scheme he had in mind, but he was in one of those moods. He wouldn't tell me. I would just have to wait and see, so I quit asking about it. I sat in the middle of the pickup seat drinking my beer. We passed one cop, but he was going the other way, and Tom wasn't driving too fast just at that moment. We got out to the plastic Indian unmolested, and Tom, once again, pulled over to the shoulder. I looked at him. He sat staring at the monument to the crass economics of the white conqueror.

"Okay," Tom said at last, "you two take the chain over there and get it ready. Then signal me."

"Come on," Pat said to me.

I got out of the pickup to follow him, even though I still had no idea what we were up to. Pat reached over into the bed of the truck and hauled out a length of chain, throwing it over his shoulder. He looked both ways down the highway and, seeing no traffic, ran like hell for the plastic Hiawatha. I ran after him. Upon reaching the big Indian, Pat slung a length of the chain around its ankles, then hooked the short end of the chain back into one of the links.

"Stretch the rest of that out," he said.

I laid the chain out on the ground, trailing it along parallel to the road. I was beginning to get it. I looked up and down the road for any sign of cars. Off to the west, I saw some headlights coming our way.

"Hey," I said.

Pat looked and saw them, too.

"Just be casual," he said. "They won't notice anything."

The car finally came up and whizzed right past us without slowing down a bit. It was followed by two more, and then a pickup coming from the other direction. No one seemed to notice anything amiss. Pat looked at me.

"Are we ready?" he asked.

"I guess so," I said, still not having been told what we were up to, even though I had guessed it by then.

Suddenly Pat made a noise, which I took to be his imitation of a hoot owl, but I couldn't be sure. Across the highway, Tom gunned the old pickup. He ground the gears. The truck moved forward, made a U-turn, and pulled beside us on the opposite shoulder before moving on ahead to stop close to the end of the chain. Pat ran for the chain. I followed. Pat dropped down on his knees, picked up the chain, and started to coil it around some part of the pickup underneath.

"Is it all right?" asked Tom from the cab.

"I guess so," I said. "He's hitching it up."

I looked nervously from one direction to the other. No one was coming. Finally Pat stood up. "Come on," he said. "Get in the truck."

He got in first, so he was in the middle of the seat this time. I piled in right behind him. All three of us twisted our heads around to look at the big plastic Indian standing there waiting to meet his doom. Tom gunned the engine. He moved the pickup ahead slowly. The chain tightened. The engine roared. The truck did not move.

"Damn it," said Tom.

"Back it up," said Pat. "Take a run."

Tom shifted into reverse and backed up more than a car length. Then he shifted back into low. He gunned the engine. He popped the clutch. The pickup leaped forward. The chain straightened. There was a sudden jerk that came near giving us all whiplash. There was a terrible noise. Suddenly we broke loose and sort of skidded ahead, sliding off the side of the road. The engine died and would not start again.

"Damn," said Tom.

We got out and looked back behind us to see the whole rear end of the pickup still chained to the plastic Indian. The rest of the vehicle was lying stupidly in the ditch. We had to walk back to Tahlequah. We thought about hitchhiking, but there was hardly any traffic that late at night, and the few cars that did pass us by paid us no attention. The next day, when the cops called Tom about his truck, found in two pieces out on Highway 51, one part of it chained to the plastic Indian, Tom said that he knew nothing about it. Someone had taken his truck.

Tom disappeared shortly after that, presumably off chasing wild horses on government land. Pat didn't come around much. He didn't have a car, and he lived quite a ways out. I went back to my job at the Cherokee Nation, wondering daily why it seemed so much like a job at some corporation owned and run by white people. In the evenings, I found myself thinking about the Cherokee Nation before Oklahoma statehood. Of course, I was imagining. I had never known it. I knew it only through stories told by my grandparents and through books I had read.

And I thought about what had happened to it in those years following 1907. Tahlequah had a Kentucky Fried Chicken with a great big bucket on the end of a pole. The road going from town out to the tribal headquarters was lined with fast food joints and a Walmart. The old historic railroad depot was a crumbling pile of bricks. Downtown, a business called Cherokee Abstracts sported a sign out front that bore a profile of an American Indian wearing a Plains-style headdress.

Our Chief was a Republican banker who had grown up in Oklahoma City, and there was one person on the tribal council who could speak Cherokee. There were still some Indian allotments left in Indian hands, but most of the land of the old Cherokee Nation was lost, owned by white people, who fenced it in and put up signs that said "No Trespassing," "No Hunting," "No Fishing," "Get the Hell Out of Here," and other such things. And way out on Highway 51, the great symbol of it all, the huge pink plastic Indian, still stood his post.

Robert Whitekiller, Reformed

It had been a while since I had seen Robert Whitekiller. Upon my return to Tahlequah after several years' absence, I was surprised, to say the least, to find him reformed. As long as I had known him, Robert had been a magnificent and incredible drunk, a veritable wild man. For instance, there was the time in South Texas when he burst through the door of a Mexican bar and asked at the top of his booming voice, "Who's the meanest son of a bitch in here?"

A terrible silence reigned. Then all eyes in the place seemed to turn toward the same man—a big, tough-looking Mexican, sitting alone, who, when he realized that he was the center of everyone's attention, calmly accepted the label put upon him and stood slowly up, and up, and up, focusing his eyes on Robert.

"Can I sit with you?" Robert asked. "I don't want to get in no trouble."

And there was that time I had just gotten home from work, and Robert stopped by my house unexpectedly. "Come on," he said. "We're going over to the house for supper."

It was always difficult for me to say no to Robert, even if I wanted to. He had been a good friend for a good long while—a great friend, I should say. I had recently confided in him some trouble I was having with someone, serious trouble, and he had asked me, "Do you want me to kill him?" I said, "Well, no, not yet, anyway," and he loaned me a .25 caliber derringer to carry in my boot. So I went with him—in his pickup truck. We had supper, Robert and I and his live-in girlfriend of the time. We also got drunk. Robert and his sweetie got into a fight.

"Robert," she said, "kiss my ass."

"I will," he said. "I have."

Then she tossed him a dime. "Call someone who gives a shit," she said.

It was getting late, but Robert went to the telephone and dialed a number. He waited for someone to answer. Then he said, "Minnie?"

Minnie was his mother. "Minnie, do you give a shit?" He hung up the phone a moment later and said, "My mother gives a shit."

It wasn't long after that I was feeling pretty woozy, and I decided anyway that I'd had about enough of their bickering, so I said to Robert, "I'm drunk. Take me home."

He tossed me his keys, saying, "I'm too drunk to drive. Take my truck."

So I did, even though I knew I was in worse shape than he was. I went home, parked Robert's pickup in my front yard, and went to bed. It must have been about three o'clock in the morning when I was awakened by a loud pounding on my front door. Sleepily, I called out, "Who is it?"

"It's me," was the reply. The voice was Robert's. "Give me my truck keys, my gun, and three dollars for a six-pack."

The drunkest I have ever been in my life was one time when I made the terrible mistake of trying to keep up with Robert Whitekiller. My sweetheart, not yet my wife, told me that before it was all over, Robert and I were running through the woods together whooping. I never could remember anything about it. But I had been away for several years, and when I returned, I found Robert reformed. He was really reformed.

His latest wife had left him, taking with her their young son, and Robert wanted them both back, especially the boy. Robert, who always managed to hold down a good job in spite of his antics, was giving them money, providing them a house, picking the boy up after school, and doing all kinds of other things. He was going to church and taking a lead role in everything that went on there. He had quit drinking. It was absolutely amazing, and I kept thinking that the universe should respond in some appropriate way, as with a monumental earthquake or something of equal impact.

Now and then, Robert called me to go with him to pick up the boy after school or go out for lunch or something. We went one time to a kids' hockey game. Robert wanted to be doing things with his son, and often he wanted me to come along for the ride. One day he asked me to go fishing with him, just the two of us. While we were lazing around on the banks of Grand Lake, sometimes known as Lake o' the

Cherokees, one of those monumental Army Corps of Engineers projects built for the leisure of white people in Tulsa at the expense of Cherokee communities and cemeteries, Robert told me that he had been having conversations with God. I said, didn't I, that he had really reformed. He asked me if I had ever talked with God.

"I suppose I have," I confessed. "At least, I've talked to him, but I don't believe he's ever answered me."

We didn't catch any fish that afternoon, but we did have a long visit, and it was good. In spite of everything, Robert was always one of my best friends. Several months went by in this way, until the day he called me up at home in the middle of the afternoon.

"I've been thinking real hard about this," he said, "and I decided that all I'm doing is being a hypocrite. I'm just an old drunk, so I'm going out to get drunk. Go with me."

"Well, okay," I said. That was probably a foolish thing to say, but I've already admitted that I always had a tough time saying no to Robert.

"I'll be right by to get you," he said, and he hung up the phone.

True to his word, Robert came by the house in his new black GMC pickup. I got in with him, and we drove downtown to the nearest bar. Red's Place was owned by another good friend of mine, and he was working behind the bar when we showed up. I ordered a bourbon and soda, and Robert ordered a shot of some kind of bourbon and a bottle of beer. Just as Red placed the shot and the bottle in front of Robert, I said, "Wait a minute, Robert."

He looked at me. "What?" he said.

"Have you talked to God about this?" I asked him.

"Yeah, I have," he said.

"What did he say?"

"He said he's gonna kick my butt," said Robert, and he picked up the shot and tossed it down in one gulp. Then he started drinking the beer. We had a few more, and Robert got progressively louder. I could tell that it was going to turn into one of those nights. I finally made an excuse and got the hell out, just leaving him there. Red told me later that he'd had to throw Robert out before long. He was getting loud and obnoxious. He was trying to start a fight with someone; he wanted to break the place up, throw people through windows, and things like that.

The next morning, I went to breakfast, as usual, at a downtown restaurant, and Robert showed up with a strange blonde. He had met her in jail, he said, and helped her out. They ordered breakfast, and we sat and talked. I asked Robert what had happened after I left him the night before.

"Your buddy threw me out," he said. So he had gone to another bar, and then to another. "I don't remember just what happened after that," he said, "but when I woke up this morning, I was in jail, and someone had stolen my pickup."

The pickup, by the way, was never recovered, and I never saw the blonde again.

How Robert Whitekiller Got a New Name and Found His Own Grave

Old man Roman White Horse was walking along a lonesome highway just off the reservation in South Dakota. He walked slowly and aimlessly until he came to a bridge that spanned a river. He walked over to the railing and stopped, looking down into the waters below. With a little effort, he lifted first one leg and then the other to swing them over the rail; then he sat on the edge, his feet dangling, with his hands on the railing beside him. He continued staring into the waters. He was broke and alone, and he did not have much time left, anyway: he was old.

A new GMC pickup came racing down the highway and came to a sudden stop there beside Roman. Roman did not bother to turn his head and look. The driver of the pickup shut off the engine and called out to him. "Hey, what you doing there?"

"Just sitting here thinking about jumping in," said Roman.

He heard the door open and then close again, and in another minute, the driver was sitting there beside him. "What you want to do that for?" he asked.

"Why not?" said Roman. "Nobody would miss me. I'm almost dead anyway."

"What about your family? You got kids?"

"Got nobody. Nobody cares."

"Well, hey," said the driver of the GMC. "My name's Robert Whitekiller, and I care."

For the first time, Roman turned his head to look at his visitor.

"You're Indian, but you ain't from around here. I never seen you before."

"I'm a Cherokee," said Robert, "from Oklahoma. Say, I got some cold beer in the truck. You want to have one?"

Roman grinned. "That sounds like a good idea."

"Stay right here now till I get back," said Robert. He swung his legs back over the rail and hurried over to his pickup. Reaching behind the seat, he brought out a small cooler and took two beers out of it. He went back to where Roman sat waiting and handed him one. They each popped open a can and took a satisfying drink.

"Ah, that's good," said the old man. "I'm glad you came by."

"Me too. Where do you live?"

"Not far. I couldn't have walked here if it was far."

"You want me to give you a ride home?"

"I just came from there. Ain't nothing there."

"Well, say, how would you like to go with me and get some hamburgers?"

"That sounds good."

They headed down the road, Robert following Roman's directions to a place where Roman said they could get good hamburgers. As they moved along, Roman asked, "What are you doing way up here from Oklahoma?"

"I'm working with a crew over here laying a pipeline. I'll be here for a while, I guess."

"Turn right here," said Roman.

Robert made a right onto a dirt road. A mile and a half later, he pulled into a large gravel parking lot in front of a low building that was covered with signs. The biggest ones said "BAR" and "STORE." Smaller signs read "Hamburgers," "Cold Beer," and "Groceries." Robert parked the pickup, and he and Roman crunched their way across the lot and went into the building. A jukebox was blaring out a country song, but the talking just about drowned it out. Robert blinked. The light was dim. At last his eyes adjusted, and he could see that the place was pretty well packed. He could also see that most of the people in the bar were Indians.

"There's a place at the bar," said Roman, and they walked over to it and sat down on stools that might have been upholstered some years back. Pretty soon a big, husky white man came over to wait on them.

"Well, hello, Roman," he said. "Who's your friend?"

"Robert Whitekiller," said Roman. "He kept me from jumping in the river."

"I ain't from around here. I'm from Oklahoma," said Robert, deciding to cut through the bullshit.

"What can I get for you?" asked the white man.

"Hamburgers and beer," said Robert.

"How many?"

"Just one at a time."

The man brought two beers and then went back to cook the hamburgers. A young Indian man with shoulder-length hair sitting on the other side of Roman leaned forward to look at Robert. "You say you're from Oklahoma?" he asked.

"That's right."

"What kind of Indian are you?"

"I'm a Cherokee," said Robert.

"I thought all Cherokees were white."

"Well, I'm here to prove you wrong about that."

"What are you, FBI?"

"Yeah: Full-Blood Indian."

The young man laughed, and then he said, "Did I hear your name right?"

"It's Robert Whitekiller," said Robert.

"Whitekiller," said the young man. "That's a hell of a good name. What did you do to earn it?"

"What are you, FBI? That's for me to know and you to find out."

The man brought the hamburgers. Robert looked at them and said, "Bring two more, and two more beers."

The young man turned around to face the big room. He stood up and called out in a loud voice, "Hey, guys, there's a real full-blood Cherokee up here, and his name is Whitekiller."

Lots of people gathered around and asked questions. Some of them slapped Robert on the back. The bar became a friendly down-home kind of place. Robert ate two hamburgers and drank four beers. Old man Roman White Horse ate six hamburgers and had six beers. Robert decided it was finally time to get going, but first he asked Roman, "Say, how long has it been since you had anything to eat?"

"I don't know. Few days."

"There's a grocery store in here. What say we grab you a few groceries before I take you home?"

"Okay."

They went into the grocery side of the bar, and Robert picked up packages of sliced ham, loaves of bread, mustard, pickles, sliced turkey, a twelve-pack of beer, peanut butter, jelly, coffee, and a few other odds and ends. "It'll be a week before I can get back around," he said. "I want to make sure you've got plenty till then."

They left the bar, and Robert drove Roman to his house. There he unloaded the groceries. He said goodbye to the old man and reminded him that he would be back in a week. He told him to stay out of trouble and wait for him. He turned to walk back out to his pickup, but the old man stopped him.

"You're the only friend I got now," he said. "That means we change names. From now on, you're Roman White Horse, and I'm Robert Whitekiller."

"Well, all right," said Robert. "I'll see you in a week, Robert."

He left the old man standing in front of his house grinning as he drove away.

Back on the job, Robert found out that they had fallen seriously behind. They worked five long days, and then they had to work the weekend. They worked the five-day week following that, and finally Robert got his weekend off. He drove back to the home of Roman White Horse. When he cut off his engine in front of the house, he was surprised the old man didn't come out to see who was there. He got out and walked to the front door. He knocked but got no answer. He yelled out for Robert Whitekiller. He peeked in a window. Finally he tried the door, found it unlocked, and walked in. He could tell that some of the groceries had been eaten. He found no sign of Roman White Horse.

He walked back out to his pickup and got in, starting the engine. He drove back to the bar where Roman had taken him before and went inside. The place was not as crowded as it had been the first time. Robert looked around, but he saw no sign of the old man. He walked over to the bar, where he was met by the big white man.

"Welcome back," the white man said. "What can I get for you?"

"I'm looking for old Roman White Horse," Robert said.

"Oh, that's right," said the white man. "You ain't been around, so you wouldn't know."

"Know what?"

"Old Roman died. Just a few days after you left."

Robert got directions to the graveyard where the old man had been laid to rest, and he drove straight over there. It didn't take long to locate the fresh grave. It had a simple marker on it that read "Robert Whitekiller." Robert felt a cold chill pass over his body, but he shrugged it off, and then he said out loud, "That's all right. I'm Roman White Horse now."

Dlanusi/Leech

Gog'ski, or Smoker, was having a big feed at Rocky Ford in the Goingsnake District of the Cherokee Nation. Rocky Ford was not a place anyone would recognize while passing through, but it was a place the Cherokees who lived there recognized as a community. The homes of the residents of Rocky Ford were scattered throughout the hills, and even when two or three families might be located within easy walking distance, or even within shouting distance, they were still not within view of each other. A near neighbor's home was always obscured from sight by the thick growth of trees, the winding roads, and the ups and downs of the Ozark foothills. What made Rocky Ford a community was purely and simply the sense of community of its inhabitants. They attended the same church, a Cherokee-language Baptist church, and they got together frequently for community gatherings. They also knew and minded each other's business as if it were their own.

Anyway, Gog'ski was having a big feed at his home. Perhaps there was an occasion for this feed, perhaps not. That information has been obscured by the passing of a century and perhaps a decade. Hogs had been slaughtered, much food had been prepared, and a large and jovial crowd had gathered around Gog'ski's log cabin. The crowd consisted mostly of full-blood Cherokees, and the conversation was all in the Cherokee language. Gog'ski was running around acting busy, playing the host, but he finally slowed down a bit to catch his breath, stopping in a small cluster of men who had been engaged in idle chatter.

"This is a good gathering," said Walkingstick to Gog'ski.

"Everyone should get plenty to eat," said Gog'ski. "There's lots of food. I killed three hogs."

"That might not be enough if Dlanusi was here," said Yudi, and his comment was answered by a round of good-natured laughter.

"Yeah," said Gog'ski, "old Leech could really put away the hog meat. Well, I guess he still can."

"He could if he could get to it," said Walkingstick. "I bet that's the worst part of jail for Dlanusi. They don't feed them much hog meat in there, I bet. Ask Shell."

"More like hog slop," said Shell, or Uyasga.

"Say," said Yudi. "You were over there in that Fort Smith jail with Leech, weren't you?"

"Uh-huh," said Shell. "For too long."

"At least they let you out," said Gog'ski. "They won't ever let Dlanusi out. Not until they hang him, I guess."

"When will they do that?" asked Yudi.

"I'm not sure," said Gog'ski, wrinkling his brow as if in deep thought. There was a pause, and then Shell spoke again. "Today," he said. Everyone looked at him.

"They're supposed to do it today," he said.

The awkward silence continued until Gog'ski stood up and paced nervously. "Today," he repeated. "I guess we shouldn't be here having such a good time. Not if they're going to hang Leech today. He could be hanging right now."

Yudi shivered, and Walkingstick looked at the ground. Gog'ski's right hand went instinctively to his own throat. He looked at Shell. "You've only been home about a week," he said. "You were in the same cell with Dlanusi, weren't you?"

"Yes, I was," said Shell.

"Did he know then when it would be his last day?"

"Yes, he knew."

"How was he?" said Gog'ski.

"What do you mean?"

"Well," said Gog'ski, "was he sad? Was he afraid?"

"No," said Shell. "He was cheerful. He joked. He seemed happier than I, even though I knew I was getting out."

Everyone was quiet then, listening to hear what more Shell might have to say. The group had gotten a little larger since the discussion of Dlanusi, the Leech, had begun.

"It was maybe seven days before I got out," said Shell. "Sgili equa, the Big Witch, came to visit Dlanusi, and he brought some soap, the kind we make at home. There was never enough soap in the stinking jail, and the guards let Dlanusi keep it. After that, he washed every day, maybe two, three times a day. He was so clean.

"The day before they let me out, Dlanusi dipped his hands in the water bucket, and he was holding his soap. Then he stood up, and he started rubbing the soap, and he lay back on his cot. He was making a lot of bubbles, and pretty soon the bubbles started to rise up and float, and Dlanusi started to laugh, a happy-sounding laugh. The bubbles were floating up and going out the window between the bars and just floating away. Dlanusi stopped laughing, but he still had a big smile on his face, and he said to me, 'You see that? I can get out of here just that easy.' Then I looked closer, and inside each bubble I could see a tiny little man sitting and smiling at me as his bubble rose up slowly and floated out the window, between the bars and away, carrying him with it. That's what I saw when I was there in jail with Dlanusi."

Shell stopped talking, and the others just sat there as if stunned. At last Gog'ski got up and clapped his hands together. "Well," he said, "does anyone want to go over there and toss some marbles with me?"

The group broke up. Some followed Gog'ski to play marbles—the old Cherokee game of marbles, more closely resembling lawn bowling than what white men call marbles; others wandered until they found someone else to talk to, perhaps to repeat the strange story Shell had just told them. Shell stayed right where he had been all along. He just sat there. Later the women called out that the food was ready, and the men all lined up to be served. They were just sitting down when a horseman came riding toward the house. All watched to see who was coming, and when he got close enough to recognize, Shell was the first one to speak. "Dlanusi," he said.

Dlanusi rode right up close. He was sitting on a shiny saddle on the back of a big black stallion that pranced and snorted, and he was dressed flashy, like a cowboy, in black leather boots and a black vest over a clean white shirt. His long black hair folded on his shoulders, and he wore a black flat-brimmed hat on his head. His broad grin showed his white teeth flashing out of his dark face. "Hey," he said, in a loud and cheerful voice, "did you leave me anything to eat here?"

Tom Starr

Tom Starr was getting old. He was at peace with himself and almost everybody else for just about the first time in his life. It was the first and only peace he could really remember. As a young man, he had lived in the old country, in North Carolina when it was still Cherokee. He had grown to huge manhood in those mountains. A tall and rangy youth, he towered over most Cherokees, and he could outrun them all in the footraces. He was known far and wide for that accomplishment.

It was the Irish blood of his father, he knew, that had made him grow so big. But the Irish blood caused other things. It made him a man not of two worlds but a man of a world all his own. He did not move from the world of the white man to that of the red. He lived in both, or parts of both, all the time. He had never known Ireland, only the Cherokee Nation. And even though his lifestyle was far from that of the conservative full-bloods, his world was Cherokee. He was made of the Irish blood that ran through the Starrs and of the Cherokee blood from his mother and his mother's mothers. His father, James, had some Cherokee blood too, but it was not much, and the only effect it seemed to have on him was to get him involved in Cherokee politics, and that had proved to be disastrous.

The Starrs had gone west, not with the Old Settlers, those who had formed the Western Cherokee Nation, or the Cherokee Nation West, as it was often called. They had gone west with the treaty signers and attempted to blend in with those who had gone before. Then the Trail of Tears happened with all its suffering, and shortly after its conclusion, the assassinations, the retaliations, the Cherokee civil war, although no one ever called it that, not quite.

It had all started when the Ross people, those who followed the lead of Principal Chief John Ross and who had, as a result, suffered over the bloody trail, began to take their revenge on those who had signed the treaty of removal. The signers had known it would happen, for Major Ridge himself, the leader of that group, had said when he put his mark on the paper, "I feel as if I have just signed my own death warrant." He knew what he was doing. Had not he himself been appointed the executioner of Doublehead some years before because of that chief's selling of Cherokee land? He knew what he was doing, but he thought that it was best for all the people.

Then, after the end of the trail, assassins got him, his son John, and his nephew Elias Boudinot, who had also signed the treaty, all on the same day, at about the same time. Some shot Major Ridge from ambush as he rode along a lonely stretch of road. Others broke into John's home, where he lay sick in his bed, and dragged him out and stabbed him many times, then took him to the yard, flung his body into the air, and stamped on it when it came down. His wife and young son looked on the whole time. A third group called Boudinot out for help, and as he walked along the path with them, others came out of the bushes and hacked him with their axes. Later, over the body, Boudinot's brother, Stand Watie, said, "I'll pay ten thousand dollars for the names of the men who did this deed."

The war was on, and Tom and his brothers, Bean and Ellis, joined in heartily. They harassed people at the polls on voting days. They robbed country stores and raided the homes of the rich Ross people, often burning them down and killing the inhabitants. Eventually, some Ross men went to the home of their father, James Starr, and killed him. Tom swore bloody revenge. Soon it was said of Tom that he had killed one hundred men.

Thinking back, he laughed at the thought. Oh, he had done his share of dirty deeds, but he had not killed one hundred men, not by a long shot. But the rumor was fun to live with. He recalled the time he and his brothers were being pursued by a large posse of Cherokee Light Horse police, and they raced toward the Arkansas border to escape them. It was looking like they would not make it, though, and Tom told Ellis and Bean to ride ahead. He turned his horse around to make sure the Light Horse saw him, and then he led them away from Ellis and Bean.

He rode into the hills, dismounted, and slapped the horse away. Then he crawled into a cave to hide. While he waited in the cave, he quietly and patiently watched a spider spinning her delicate, intricate web across the opening. Soon the posse was just outside. Huddled back in the darkness, Tom heard one say, "They found his horse just over there without a rider. He can't be far."

"Here," said another. "Look in this cave."

From his spot in the black interior, Tom could see them bend over to look inside, and he heard one of them say, "He can't be in there. No one's been in there for a long time. See, the entrance is covered by spider webs." And then they went on their way.

When peace was at last made between the warring factions, the Starrs had been so notorious for their activities that they continued to be hunted as outlaws. Bean and Ellis had at last been killed by the Light Horse, but Tom continued his outlaw career. He stole horses in the Cherokee Nation and sold them in Texas, and he stole Texans' horses and sold them to Cherokees. When his son Sam was grown, he joined in the family business.

But Sam was a source of constant worry to old Tom. He was cocky and spoiled, reckless but not brave. Sam was a constant disappointment to Tom, for Tom could not find one single thing about the snotty young man to admire. Without Tom to protect him, Sam would not last long in the family business. Tom recalled that affair with Bill West of a few years back, and he knew that Sam would never have been able to deal with it, or with anything like it. Bill had been Tom's brother-in-law. Even so, Tom had never liked the man.

Bill had not been a good husband to Tom's sister, and Tom had only tolerated him for his sister's sake. But the time finally came when Bill went just too far. He had mistreated his wife once too often, and on top of that, he insulted Tom in public, in front of people Tom respected. Bill was a white man, as big as Tom, and he was a brutal man, a man never known to have been beaten in a fight.

Tom faced him and pulled out his long knife. "Bill, you've gone too far this time," he said.

Bill looked at him and grinned, a wide and sneering grin, and he too drew a knife. He held it in his right hand out in front of him, and with his left, he gestured at Tom to come ahead. "Let's get it on, then, Tom," he said. "This has been coming for a while."

They made false moves at one another, each one testing the other, feeling the other out. Bill made a sudden sweeping slash intended to gut Tom, but Tom sprang back just in time to avoid the cut. Bill stepped back quickly. He turned the knife over in his hand and raised it over his head for a downward thrust, and when he made the move, Tom stepped back again. This time, though, he stepped back in at once, and with his left hand he caught Bill's right wrist. With his own right, he made an upward thrust. The knife blade dug deep into the chest of Bill West.

Bill struggled, but Tom kept pushing with all his strength. The blood pumped out of Bill's chest, running down his shirt front, running over Tom's clenched fist on the hilt of the knife, running down Tom's sleeve to his elbow, dripping off and puddling on the ground. Bill looked into Tom's eyes with a cold hatred that soon melted to disbelief and despair and then went blank. His huge body relaxed. His knees buckled, and Tom withdrew the knife as the body crumpled to the ground. There would be no more trouble with Bill West.

After wiping the knife blade clean on Bill's clothes, Tom turned as if to walk away. Then he hesitated. He recalled that there was a large reward offered for Bill by the Cherokee Nation. It would be a terrible waste, he thought, to just let the body lie and rot or be eaten by crows and coyotes. He turned back and knelt, and quickly and expertly, he severed the head from the body. Then he mounted his horse for the ride into Tahlequah, the capital city.

It was a bold thing he did that day, perhaps as bold a thing as he had ever done or ever would do. No one would have thought much of Tom's taking his brother-in-law's head in to claim the reward except for one fact: there was also a reward for Tom Starr, and it was even larger than the one offered for Bill. Even so, Tom rode brazenly into Tahlequah and tied his horse there in front of the government offices. Carrying the grisly trophy by the hair, he walked inside. Stepping into the office of the treasurer, he held the head out for all to see. "Here is what's left of Bill West," he said. "I've come for the reward."

The disbelieving clerk filled out a paper with trembling hand for Tom to sign, and then he called into the office of the treasurer. When the treasurer stepped out, the clerk handed him the paper. The treasurer looked up at Tom with wide eyes. He went back into his office and came out a moment later with the cash, which he handed to the clerk. The clerk handed it to Tom, and Tom held out the head. The clerk recoiled, backing away from the nasty thing, revolted. Tom shrugged and placed the sorry bloody head on the edge of the desk. Then he turned and, without looking back once, walked out of the office, out of the building, and mounted his horse again.

Inside the building someone said, "Do you know who that is?"

"It's Tom Starr," was the answer.

"He's just collected the reward for Bill West."

"But the price on him is even higher, isn't it?"

"Yes, but who's fool enough to try to collect it?"

"He's made a monkey out of the whole Cherokee Nation."

Tom rode back home unmolested, feeling smug satisfaction at having openly challenged the government of Chief John Ross and emerged victorious.

⌒～〜⟆

But now Tom was old. His hair was white. He figured that he did not have much longer to live on this earth. He did not know where he would go after his life had ended. He did not know whether he even believed in the existence of a soul. His Cherokee ancestors would have told him that his soul would go to the Darkening Land in the West. He knew the stories, at least some of them. His Irish Catholic ancestors would likely have said that his soul would burn in hell for all of his evil deeds. Tom didn't really give a damn about all that. He'd had a long and mostly satisfying life. It had been a violent life, and yet he was headed for a quiet end in his old age. That in itself was quite an accomplishment.

The only thing that had come close to it in his life was when the Cherokee Nation had finally offered him amnesty if he would promise to quit his nefarious activities. He had agreed, and the rumor had grown up around him that he was the only individual ever to sign a treaty with the Cherokee Nation. It was untrue, of course. But he did have amnesty. He had accepted it, and in turn, he had given his promise. And after the agreement, Tom settled down. He stopped killing, even though he did not yet actually have a hundred men to his credit. He stopped stealing horses, although Sam was still very much engaged in that enterprise. Tom sort of retired, but he knew that he would not soon be forgotten.

He was confident in that thought at least until the white woman came around. Sam brought her. Her name was Myra Belle Shirley. She was a known associate of Cole Younger, and she was part of the horse-stealing ring that had grown up around Sam. She was typical of the gang that Sam had cultivated. From Missouri originally, she had a brother who had been with Quantrill's Raiders during the War Between the States. They had associated themselves with Stand Watie, who had become not just the only Indian general in the Confederate Army, but also the last of them all to surrender. They had also been associated with Jesse James and his brother Frank and with Cole Younger and his brothers. Not knowing anything but fighting, after the war they had all become outlaws. And although Tom doubted the story, Myra Belle was rumored to have been a Confederate spy. He did not doubt that her little daughter Pearl was the daughter of Cole Younger.

But the worst of it all was that Sam had married Myra Belle, or at least she had moved in with him, and he called her his wife. It didn't really matter one way or the other, for she was now widely known as Belle Starr. She was becoming notorious as the Outlaw Queen. There were fanciful books being written about her. She was hailed as the head of a vast gang of horse thieves and murderers—she, not Sam. And Tom Starr could already see, toward the end of his long and event-filled life, that he would soon be forgotten, his memory washed away by hers. The whole Starr family and their connection to the Cherokee Nation would be forgotten. Their fame and notoriety would be eclipsed by the legend that was growing up around that horribly ugly white woman who was already semi-famous as the Outlaw Queen, Belle Starr.

The Funeral of Charlie Wickliffe

The Wickliffe brothers were notorious. They were always together, and they were being hounded by the United States Marshals, but the curious thing is that only Charlie, the oldest, was wanted for any crime, and more curious was the fact that the only crime for which he was wanted was the killing of deputy U.S. marshals. No one seemed to know just why Charlie had killed that first marshal. The rest was easy, of course. The second and third and so on had come after him for killing the first one and the second one and on and on. But then the strangest thing of all occurred. The two younger Wickliffe brothers, John and Tom, appeared in Tahlequah one day when the deputy marshals were there and identified themselves.

"John and Tom Wickliffe," said the deputy. "I'll be damned. Where's Charlie?"

"Charlie's dead," said John. "I killed him."

"You killed your brother? How come you to do that?"

"We just got in a fuss about something, and it turned to a fight and she got killed. That's all."

"You killed him?"

"We come to turn ourselfs in."

"Well, now, you two aren't wanted for anything. We got no warrants on you, just on Charlie."

"You ain't gonna put us in jail?"

"No."

"Not even me for killing Charlie?"

"It's not against the law to kill a wanted man."

"You mean we can go home now?"

"Well, yeah, except I got to ask you something. Where's the body? You know I can't close this case just on your word. I've got to see the body for official identification."

"We gonna have the funeral tomorrow afternoon. You can come up there if you want to."

"Well, all right. I'll do that."

Family and friends were gathered at the cemetery near the Wickliffe home. A fresh grave had been dug, and a casket was ready to be lowered. They were singing Cherokee hymns, and people were crying. The deputy marshals came riding up, dismounted, and tied their horses. They walked over near to the grave. There was praying and preaching in the Cherokee language, and it seemed to the deputies to be interminable. At last the casket was going to be lowered.

"Hold on a minute," said one of the deputies. Everything stopped. No one spoke. "We need to see the body."

"You mean you want to open up that casket?" said John Wickliffe.

"We've got to see him," said the deputy.

John put a hand on the lawman's shoulder and walked with him away from the crowd. "Listen," he said, "I shot Charlie right in the face. That body's a mess. We done sealed up that coffin so my mother wouldn't have to look at her like that. That's Mother right there standing by the grave." He gestured toward an elderly Cherokee woman who was streaming tears. "You can see the funeral going on here, the whole family and all the friends. See them crying. You heard the preacher talking and praying. That body ain't smelling none too good just now, either, and we got to put her under the ground."

The deputy walked over to his two companions, and they huddled together for a moment. Then he walked back over to where John waited. "Go on with what you got to do," he said. "We'll just say we attended the funeral." He went back to his partners, and they walked to their horses, mounted up, and rode away. The coffin was lowered into the ground, and someone started shoveling dirt into the hole. When the deputies were well away, Charlie Wickliffe stepped out of the woods.

"Ole Lester's hog got a hell of a good sending off, didn't she?" he said, and everyone burst into hearty laughter.

⌒〜⤴

Editor's Note: The play on words (gender terms) in this story is reminiscent of Cherokee humor at its best.

Beehunter Saves the Day

Beehunter sat on a cane-bottomed chair in front of his small log cabin at the base of Bald Hill in the Tahlequah District of the Cherokee Nation. He appeared to be aimlessly whittling on a small piece of walnut, but a closer look would reveal that he was involved in the intricate process of carving a small bear. The bear was on its hind legs, reaching up the trunk of a tree. Beehunter was not on duty with Sheriff Go-Ahead Rider, for whom he worked occasionally as a special deputy. He had not, in fact, been called on for some time. Things must have been quiet in Tahlequah, he thought.

He'd had time to do some hunting, and he had supplied his wife, Nani, with plenty of venison. He had even caught a fine batch of craw-dads, but they had eaten them already. As he sat carving, Nani was off to one side of the cabin cooking some fresh catfish he had caught just that morning. He hadn't worked for Sheriff Go-Ahead Rider for a while, but they were doing all right. They had not gone hungry.

And Beehunter seldom needed money. The small garden, his hunting and fishing, and a few fruit trees provided them all the food they needed. In fact, they almost always had enough to give some away to others. He grew and cured his own tobacco. He did like coffee, though, and he thought it wise to always have a good supply of shells for his old shotgun. They came in handy when he needed some meat for the table.

He sat and he carved, smelling the catfish cooking just around the corner, and it smelled good. Nani was a fine cook, a good woman. He was proud of his wife, and just now, he was anxious to be tasting the catfish she cooked. After he had cleaned the fish for her, she cut the meat in small strips and dropped them in hot grease in a big iron pot over an open fire. Thinking about it and smelling the odors from around the corner made him hungry.

But there was something else, a feeling, something he could not quite put words to, that was nagging at him as he sat there. He felt like someone would be coming to see him soon. He couldn't tell who it would be, but he felt as if it had something to do with Go-Ahead Rider. Rider not only called on Beehunter for help now and then, which gave Beehunter almost the only money he ever made, but Rider was a good friend. Beehunter had often said that there was no better man alive than Go-Ahead Rider.

"The fish is cooked," Nani called out. She spoke in Cherokee, her only language. Beehunter could speak both Cherokee and Creek, but he, like his wife, could speak no English. Oh, he could understand when someone said "Hello," and he recognized his own name and that of Rider when he heard them spoken in English, but that was about all. He sliced a bit of surplus wood off the nose of his bear and set the carving aside.

"I'm coming," he said. He stood up and folded his pocketknife. Dropping it in a pocket, he looked up to see a rider leading an extra horse headed toward his house. "Someone coming to see us," he said. He walked toward the corner of his cabin, and Nani stepped away from the cooking pot, wiping her hands on her apron. She met him there and looked toward the rider in the distance.

"Who is it?" she asked.

"I don't know yet," he said, but he thought, it's something to do with Rider. Nani turned away from him and walked back to her fire. Beehunter stood staring at the distant figure slowly growing larger in his vision. She came back and handed him a piece of fish.

"It's hot," she said.

He took it and took a bite. It was hot. He chewed fast and swallowed it down. "Good," he said. "*Wado.*" He put the rest of it into his mouth and chewed it. It was almost as hot as the first bite had been, and it was just as good. "It's Earl Bob," he said. He didn't bother saying it, but he could also tell that Earl Bob was leading the little roan from the sheriff's stable that Beehunter liked to ride.

"Yes," said Nani. "I can see him now. Maybe Rider wants you to come to work."

"Maybe," said Beehunter.

Earl Bob was another of Rider's occasional deputies. He got more work than did Beehunter because he could speak both Cherokee and English, and even though Tahlequah was the capital city of the

Cherokee Nation, there were more and more people there who could not speak Cherokee. Rider had tried several times to get Beehunter a full-time job. Beehunter knew that. But the chief or the council or the judge or whoever made the decisions wouldn't let him do it, because Beehunter could not speak any English. Nani brought him another piece of fish, and he ate it. Earl Bob was almost close enough by then to yell at, but Beehunter just ate his fish and waited.

Soon Earl Bob rode up close to the cabin. "*Siyo*, Beehunter," he said. He touched the brim of his hat. "*Siyo*, Nani. *Tohiju?*"

"*Uh, tohigwu*," said Nani. "*Nihina?*"

"I'm all right, too," Earl Bob said. "Thanks."

"Get down," said Beehunter, and Earl Bob swung down out of his saddle, allowing the reins of both animals to trail on the ground. Nani disappeared around the corner of the house. Beehunter indicated an extra chair, and Earl Bob sat down. Beehunter sat in the chair he had been in before.

"You carving?" Earl Bob asked him.

Beehunter picked up his bear and handed it to Earl Bob. "It's not finished," he said. Earl Bob turned the bear around and around, studying all the details. "It's looking pretty good," he said. "What's he doing? Looking for honey?"

Beehunter chuckled, and just then Nani came around the corner of the house and handed each man a tin cup full of coffee. "*Wado*," said Earl Bob.

"There's catfish, too," she said, and she disappeared again. Beehunter looked at the little roan. He wondered just what Earl Bob had ridden all the way out there to tell him, but he didn't say anything. Earl Bob would tell him soon enough. Nani came back with two plates, each piled high with pieces of beautifully fried catfish. She handed one to Earl Bob and the other to her husband. Earl Bob thanked her again, and she went back around to her fire. For a few moments, the two men ate in silence.

"Exie came by the sheriff's office this morning," Earl Bob said. "Rider didn't go home last night. He didn't show up at the office this morning, either. He went over to Muskogee to take that white man prisoner to Marshal Lovely, you know, and he should have come home the night before last. We thought maybe something happened over there to hold him up for another day, so we weren't worried about him until Exie came by. She said he should be home by now."

"He's probably just taking a little while longer than he thought he would," Beehunter said. "Maybe he had more business with that white lawman than he thought."

"That's what I told Exie," said Earl Bob. "She said that he should have been back even yesterday, but he told her he would be back last night at the latest. She's worried about him."

Nani appeared at the corner of the cabin with a look of deep concern on her face. "Exie doesn't worry like that for nothing," she said.

Beehunter stuffed the last piece of fish from his plate into his mouth and gulped it down. He wiped his fingers on his britches and stood up. "I'll go find him," he said. He picked up his coffee cup and drained it. Then he turned to his wife. "I have to go now, Nani," he said. "Rider might be in some trouble."

"Wait," she said, and she hurried into the house.

"I brought the roan for you," Earl Bob said. "And the guns you like. I hope you don't need them."

Beehunter walked over to the roan and checked the saddle boot for the single-shot Warner carbine. It was there. The Smith & Wesson .44 American revolver was in its holster, the belt buckled and slung over the saddle horn. Beehunter took it and strapped it around his waist. "Me too," he said, and he swung himself easily up into the saddle.

Nani came out of the house with a bundle in a white cloth. She hurried around the corner to her fire.

Earl Bob finished his catfish and his coffee and stood up. Turning toward Nani, he said, "Thank you. The catfish was good. The coffee, too."

Beehunter was already turning the roan to ride out when Earl Bob got into his saddle. "I don't know how long this will take," Beehunter said over his shoulder.

"Be careful," Nani said, hurrying over to his side. She opened a flap on his saddlebag and stuffed the bundle down into it. "Some food," she said.

Then the two men rode off together. They were halfway across the field before Beehunter spoke again. "Who is this white man prisoner?" he asked. "What did he do?"

"He's a whiskey seller," said Earl Bob. "Rider's been after him for some time now. He finally found out who was bringing all that whiskey in from Arkansas, and he caught him, but he's a white man, so Rider had to take him over to Marshal Lovely."

"Was Rider on his big black horse?" Beehunter asked.

"Yes," said Earl Bob.

"This white man," said Beehunter, "Rider's prisoner, what was he called?"

"He called himself Chunk Harlan," said Earl Bob.

Beehunter said the name over and over again to himself, trying to set the uncomfortable English sounds in his brain. "Chunk Hollan. Chunk Hollan," he said. Then out loud to Earl Bob he said, "What does this Chunk Hollan look like?"

"He's a bit shorter than you," Earl Bob said. (Beehunter was five feet, seven inches tall.) "He's heavy, though. Solid built. He has yellow hair and a yellow stubby beard. His arms are hairy, too. Also yellow. His eyes are very light blue, and his skin is white, but red shows through. It's ugly."

Beehunter nodded and grunted. "Chunk Hollan," he said.

When they reached the road to Muskogee and Earl Bob turned to ride into Tahlequah, Beehunter rode along with him.

"Aren't you going to Muskogee?" Earl Bob asked.

"I'm going somewhere else first," said Beehunter. "Then Muskogee."

Earl Bob didn't ask any more questions. They rode quietly the rest of the way into Tahlequah. When Earl Bob turned to ride back to the jail, Beehunter turned in the opposite direction. He rode out of town a few miles, then moved onto a trail that wound through the thick woods. Before long, he came up to a small cabin. An old Cherokee man was sitting in front of the cabin smoking a pipe. He smiled as Beehunter stopped his horse.

"Welcome," he said. "Come down."

Beehunter dismounted and walked over to the old man, who offered him a chair. Beehunter sat down and took off his hat.

"White Tobacco," he said, "I've come about Go-Ahead."

"What's the trouble?" White Tobacco asked.

"Go-Ahead went to Muskogee with a white man, his prisoner,"

Beehunter said. "He was taking the white man to the white lawman over there. He hasn't come home, and his wife is worried about him."

White Tobacco sat for a while in silence looking thoughtful. At last he stood up and walked into his house without saying anything. Beehunter waited patiently. From a branch overhead in a large white oak tree, a squirrel chattered angrily and a blue jay screeched. A small green lizard ran up on top of a rock nearby and seemed to be looking at Beehunter. White Tobacco came back out of the house and sat down again.

"I looked in my crystal," he said. "Go-Ahead's in trouble."

"I have to look for him," Beehunter said.

White Tobacco opened up his hand to reveal a wad of string with a small stone tied to one end. He found the loose end of the string and held it up so that the stone dangled, and he sat still and watched it dangle for a time. Then the stone seemed to move and point directly west. "He's that way," the old man said.

Beehunter thought it strange, for Muskogee was southwest. If he were to ride directly west, he would be going toward Wagoner. Both towns were in the Creek Nation, but that didn't matter to Beehunter. He wasn't acting as a deputy sheriff anyhow. He was a private citizen, looking for his friend who might be in trouble. And he could talk to Creeks. It was only white men who gave him problems. He just wondered what Rider was doing over there. He thanked White Tobacco, handed him a pouch of tobacco he had grown himself, mounted the roan, and left. He headed for Wagoner.

When the sun was low in the western sky and the day was growing dim, Beehunter had not yet reached the Halfway House at Fourteen Mile Creek. That was all right with him, though. He didn't have the money to spend a night in the Halfway House, nor to eat a meal there. He stopped beside the road and unsaddled the little roan. There was good grass for her to eat, and there was a clear stream nearby. He dug into the saddlebag to see what Nani had given him for the trail, and he was pleased to find that she had wrapped up some of the catfish for him. It was good even cold. He ate a piece with some of the bread she had put in there, and then finished his meal with a peach. It would have been nice to have coffee, but he would just have to do without. He led the roan down to the stream, and they both had a drink. Then he settled down for the night.

He was up early the next morning. He was hungry, so he had some more bread and catfish. Then he saddled the roan and headed for the Halfway House. As he rode up to the establishment, he saw that there were a number of horses tied up to the hitching rail. Effie's business is good, he thought. He found room for the roan, dismounted, and lapped the reins around the rail. Then he walked inside.

The main room was crowded with people having their breakfast there. He could smell the coffee and longed for a cup, but he tried to put that out of his mind. He looked the crowd over, trying to find a familiar face. He recognized Effie Crittenden, of course. She owned the place. But he knew that she spoke only English, so he couldn't talk to her. He finally found one Cherokee man to talk to, but the man had not seen Go-Ahead Rider and did not know Chunk "Hollan." He found a Creek man he knew only slightly and tried him.

"Chunk Hollan," the Creek said. "The whiskey man?"

"Yes," said Beehunter, speaking in the Muskogee tongue. "You know him?"

"I know him," the man said.

Beehunter grew more anxious then. "Have you seen Chunk Hollan?" he asked.

The man shook his head. "I haven't seen him for some time," he said, "but I heard that Go-Ahead Rider arrested him over in Tahlequah. Hey, can Rider arrest a white man?"

Beehunter rode on toward Wagoner, hoping that he would encounter more people he could talk to, and hoping for some sign of Go-Ahead Rider or of Chunk "Hollan." He saw several people along the road, and a few of them he was able to converse with, but no one knew anything about Rider or Harlan. It was late evening when he reached Wagoner. He rode around the town until it was almost dark, looking for any sign of Rider, but he saw none. He talked to a few more people but learned nothing. He rode to a stream just outside of town and made himself a camp for the night.

Early the next morning, Beehunter was walking the streets of Wagoner. At each place of business, he poked his head in to see who he could see. He had come to the end of a street where a stable stood, and he was about to cross the street and check the businesses on the other side when he glanced inside the stable door toward the stalls in there, and he saw the head of a big black horse looking over a stall gate. He could hardly believe his eyes. He thought that he must be wrong, but he went inside to be sure.

As he walked up close to the stall, he knew that he was looking at the big black stallion Go-Ahead Rider had taken on his trip to Muskogee. And here it was in Wagoner. Old White Tobacco had been right: Rider was in Wagoner. The stableman approached, and Beehunter tried to speak to him in Creek and in Cherokee, but the man kept replying with gibberish. Beehunter knew that it was English, of course, but it meant nothing to him. Finally he walked out in disgust.

He was looking up and down the street for an Indian to approach to use as an interpreter when he spotted Marshal Lovely. He hurried toward the marshal. Lovely looked to see who was coming at him so fast and recognized Beehunter. "Howdy, Beehunter," he said. "What are you doing over here?"

Beehunter, of course, understood nothing beyond the first two words. "Rider," he said.

"Rider?" said Lovely. "Rider was supposed to have showed up in Muskogee three days ago. He never showed up. Is he here?"

Beehunter didn't understand any of that. He pointed at his own chest, then at his eyes, then moved his fingers away from his eyes and said, "Rider."

Lovely squinted his own eyes, trying to figure out Beehunter's sign language. "You're looking for Rider?" he said.

Beehunter gestured for Lovely to follow him, then led the way to the stable. He took Lovely to the stall that held the black stallion. The stableman was beside them in an instant. "What's that Indian telling you about that horse?" the man said. "He was in here a few minutes ago looking at it, but he can't talk no English."

"Where'd you get that horse?" Lovely asked.

"Bought him," the man said.

"When?" said Lovely.

"Now, hold on," the man said, "just what the—"

Lovely pulled aside the lapel of his coat to reveal the badge on his vest. "I'm a U.S. marshal," he said. "When did you buy that horse?"

"Yesterday," the man said. "Just yesterday. Anything wrong?"

"Unless that horse was sold to you by Sheriff Go-Ahead Rider of the Cherokee Nation," Lovely said, "it's stolen."

"Oh, say," the man said, "I don't know nothing about that. A man came in here wanting to sell a horse. That's all I know."

"You get a bill of sale?" asked the marshal.

"Yeah," the man said. "Sure. I'll fetch it. You want me to fetch it?"

"Yeah. Fetch it," Lovely said.

The man ran for his office, and Lovely and Beehunter looked at one another. Lovely crossed his arms over his chest. Beehunter put a hand on the black horse's head. "Rider," he said. Lovely nodded. "I know," he answered. "Goddamn it, Beehunter, I wish I could talk to you."

The stableman came back from the office with a piece of paper in his hand. He stuck it in front of Lovely's face. Lovely backed off and jerked the paper from the man's hand. He turned it around to read it. "Calvin Brown," he read. "That the name of the man who sold you this horse?"

"That's the name he gave me," the man said.

"What does this Calvin Brown look like?"

"I don't know," the man said. "He's about as tall as this Indian here. Maybe a little shorter. Light hair and eyes. Kind of a heavy fellow, you know."

Lovely handed the paper back to the man, then shook a finger in his face. "You hold on to this horse," he said. "I'll be back, and if this horse is gone, you'll wind up in federal prison."

"He'll be here, marshal," the man said. "You can count on that."

Lovely motioned for Beehunter to follow him, and he led the way to a nearby café. Inside he selected a table, and the two men sat down. A waitress came over. "Can I help you?" she asked.

"Two cups of black coffee," said the marshal. "You know if anyone in here can talk both Cherokee and English?"

"That's a Cherokee man over there in the corner," she said. "He talks English to me, but I think he can talk Cherokee."

Lovely glanced over his shoulder. He saw the Indian man in the corner. He was seated alone at a table sipping coffee. "We'll join him,"

Lovely said. He got up and motioned for Beehunter to follow. At the table in the corner, Lovely said, "Excuse me, sir. I'm Marshal Lovely. This is Beehunter. Do you mind if we sit with you for a bit?"

The man seemed puzzled, but he said, "No."

Lovely and Beehunter sat down.

"I'm Guy Cornshucks," the man said. "What do you want?"

The waitress brought two cups and a coffeepot. She filled a cup for Lovely and one for Beehunter, and she refilled Cornshucks's cup. Beehunter thought the coffee sure did smell good. He picked up the cup and sipped the hot liquid.

"My friend here doesn't speak any English," said Lovely, "and I can't talk Cherokee. Can you help us?"

"Oh," said Cornshucks. "Yeah. I do what I can."

"Good. Then tell him for me that—no, ask him why he came to Wagoner."

Cornshucks asked the question of Beehunter and waited for Beehunter's answer. Then he said to Lovely, "He say he come looking for Sheriff Go-Ahead Rider. He say Rider didn't come back to Tahlequah when he should. They worried about him over there. His wife worried. He came looking for him."

"But Rider was supposed to have come to Muskogee," Lovely said. "Why did he come to Wagoner?"

Beehunter's answer to that one was vague. He did not think it was wise to tell a white lawman that an old Indian had dangled a stone at the end of a string, and Beehunter had followed the direction the stone sent him. Lovely chose not to pursue the issue. "All right," he said. "Tell him that a man who calls himself Calvin Brown sold Rider's horse to the stableman. The description of Brown that the stableman gave me sounded like Chunk Harlan."

Cornshucks repeated that information to Beehunter, and Beehunter said in Cherokee, "Hollan sold Go-Ahead's horse. That means Rider is in trouble. I've got to find him. Tell this white man that I have to go. I have to find Hollan and Go-Ahead."

Beehunter was halfway out of his chair, but Lovely put a hand around his arm to hold him. He looked at Cornshucks, and Cornshucks gave a hurried translation of Beehunter's words.

"Tell him to hold on a minute," Lovely said. "We're working together here."

Cornshucks conveyed the message, and Beehunter settled back down.

"What we have to do," Lovely said, "is ask around town after the whereabouts of Harlan. I'll get some help over at the sheriff's office. We'll check the hotels. If he was here, someone had to see him."

Again Cornshucks translated for Beehunter. Beehunter tipped up his cup and drained it of coffee. He put the cup down and stood up. "*Howa*," he said. "Let us go, then."

"He said okay, let's go," Cornshucks told Lovely.

Lovely stood up, a little disgusted that Beehunter seemed to be ordering him around, or maybe he was allowing himself to be ordered around by Beehunter. "Thanks," he said to Cornshucks. "I'll pay for your coffee."

"You want me to go along with you?" Cornshucks asked.

Lovely hesitated only a second. "Well, yeah," he said. "Sure. If you don't mind."

"If I minded I wouldn't have said so," Cornshucks said, getting up from his chair.

Outside, Lovely looked up and down the busy street. "Why don't we separate," he said, "since you're along to interpret for Beehunter. You go down that way. I'll go this way. When we get to the end of this street, if we haven't spotted Harlan yet, we'll cross the street and come back this way until we meet."

"What if we spot him?" Cornshucks said.

"If you spot him," said Lovely, "leave Beehunter to watch him, nothing more. Make him understand that. Just watch him while you come and find me. You got all that?"

"I got it good," said Cornshucks, and he began to repeat it all in Cherokee for Beehunter as Lovely started on his own way down the street.

It was half an hour later when Lovely was about to turn into a hotel just ahead. A man came out the front door. He was short and stocky and pale. He had blond hair and watery blue eyes. His shirt sleeves were rolled up, and Lovely could see that his arms were covered in light blond hair. The man wore boots, and his pant legs were tucked inside the boots. He wore a vest that seemed almost too small for his frame, and on his head was a low-crowned, wide, flat-brimmed hat. He was puffing a short cigar. He stepped out onto the sidewalk, stopped, hooked his thumbs into his waistband, and looked down into the street, as if he were waiting for someone. Hanging just under his arm was a Smith & Wesson .45.

Lovely walked a little closer. "Mr. Calvin Brown?" he said.

The man's head jerked around, and his watery eyes focused on Lovely. "You talking to me?" the man said.

"You Calvin Brown?" Lovely asked.

"No," said the man.

"Did you sell a black horse to the livery stable here using the name of Calvin Brown?" Lovely asked.

"You got the wrong man, buster," said the stocky man.

"Maybe I should call you Chunk Harlan," Lovely said. "Are you Chunk Harlan?"

"Go bother someone else," the man said. "I've got business."

"Whiskey business?" Lovely asked.

"I don't know what you're talking about. Who are you, anyhow?" the man said.

"I'm Deputy United States Marshal Lovely, and I'm asking you to walk down to the stable with me. We'll find out if you sold that black horse. If you're the wrong man, I'll apologize to you, and you'll be on your way."

"I ain't got time for that, deputy," the man said. "All right, all right. I sold the horse, but I ain't the man you're looking for."

"What's your name, mister?" Lovely said.

Some way down the street, headed east, Beehunter walked with Cornshucks. They had not come across anyone who fit the description of Chunk "Hollan." Cornshucks had asked a few questions of people they met, and they had talked to a couple of Creeks and one other Cherokee. Beehunter had an uneasy feeling, though. Just then, the image of the small stone on the end of the piece of string dangling from the fingers of old White Tobacco came back into his mind. He saw the stone as it seemed to strain to reach out toward the west.

"Come on," he said to Cornshucks in Cherokee. "We're going the wrong direction."

"But the white catcher told us to go this way," Cornshucks said.

"I have to go west," said Beehunter, and he turned to walk in the opposite direction, to the west. Cornshucks set a fast pace. He wasn't looking anymore. He was just hurrying past everyone. It didn't matter to him, for they were only retracing their steps anyway. They reached the place where they had parted company with Lovely, on the sidewalk there in front of the place where they'd had coffee, and Beehunter kept going. Cornshucks walked with him.

They hadn't gone much farther when Beehunter saw Lovely standing on the sidewalk ahead. In another instant, he saw the other man, and just as he saw the man, just as his mind registered the man's looks and the description of "Hollan," he saw the man reach for a revolver at his side. He felt a moment of panic as he watched Lovely pull out his own revolver at his side. He watched as the man he knew as "Hollan" clutched at his belly and slowly leaned forward. He watched "Hollan" crumble and fall, and he ran toward Lovely.

When Beehunter and Cornshucks reached Lovely, the deputy was kneeling beside the body of the other man. He looked up into the face of Beehunter. "I'm sorry," he said. "He didn't give me any other choice. He's dead."

"I want Rider's horse," Beehunter said, and Cornshucks repeated the words in English.

Lovely stood up slowly. "What for?" he said.

After Cornshucks translated for Beehunter, Beehunter said, "Rider will need him."

"Look," said Lovely, "I've got some things to do here yet. I have to make a report on this mess and have this body taken care of. I'll talk to the clerk inside and find out if this man was registered here, and if so, under what name. I'll ask questions about him. We'll try to trace his movements and see if we can find Rider that way."

Cornshucks did his best to relay all that to Beehunter, and Beehunter nodded his head in understanding. He had worked with Go-Ahead Rider enough to know how lawmen went about their business. "I want the horse," he said. "I'm going west."

Lovely sighed when he heard the words from Cornshucks. "All right," he said. "I'll get the horse for you."

Beehunter rode out of town alone. He was leading the big black horse. He had no knowledge of his destination. He knew only what he had learned from White Tobacco, that Rider was somewhere west. For a mile or so along the road, there were too many tracks to make sense of any of them, but then the tracks thinned out. The ones that were there were easier to see, easier to read, and Beehunter knew the tracks of the black horse well. He studied the ground closely as he rode along, and then he saw them. Some were headed west, others back east. He watched them closely, and in a while, he made the determination that the tracks headed east were the most recent. The black horse had gone west out of town, and then it had gone back to town.

Beehunter knew that "Hollan" had sold the horse in town, and so he figured that Rider had not ridden it back to town. He also knew, because of White Tobacco, that Rider was somewhere west, so he figured further that Rider had been on the horse when it made the tracks headed west. He kept riding, kept watching the tracks.

Back in Wagoner, Lovely had just finished giving the local sheriff a full report on what happened and why it happened. The body had been taken care of, and Lovely went back to the hotel where he had encountered Harlan. He went inside and walked up to the front desk. The clerk behind the desk looked up. "Can I help you?" he asked.

"I'm Deputy Marshal Lovely," said the lawman. "You hear the commotion here a while ago?"

"How could I miss it?" the man said.

"Yeah," said Lovely. "That man that got killed, did you see who it was?"

"I seen him," the clerk said.

"Well?" Lovely said. "You know him? Was he registered here?"

"Yes," said the clerk. "To both questions."

"What name was he registered under?" the deputy asked.

"Calvin Brown," said the clerk, with a silly grin on his face.

"And do you know if that was his right name?" said Lovely.

"I do," said the clerk.

"Well?"

"It ain't," the clerk said.

"So what the hell was his right name?" asked Lovely, his voice beginning to show irritation with the clerk.

"He was Chunk Harlan," the man said.

"Now, listen to me. You ain't on no witness stand, and I ain't no lawyer. You're going to start telling me everything you know without me having to drag it out of you one word at a time. You got that? Because if you let a man register under a false name, and you knew it was a false name, you broke the law. Did you know that? And if you don't give me answers, I'm going to place you under arrest and take you over to jail in Muskogee. Understand?"

The silly expression on the clerk's face had vanished. It was replaced by a serious look, a little frightened. "Yes, sir," the clerk said. "What do you want to know?"

A few miles west, the tracks in the road told Beehunter more. The big black horse had gone west in the company of five other horses. It had gone back to Wagoner with only one other horse. Rider had been with five other men, "Hollan" and four more. They must have captured him somehow. Then they had taken him somewhere west of Wagoner, and "Hollan" had taken the horse back to town to sell. That could only mean one of two things: either they had killed Rider or they meant to kill him. Beehunter's mission took on more urgency.

He tried to recall the exact words of White Tobacco. The old man had said, "Go-Ahead's in trouble." Beehunter wondered if that meant Rider was still alive. Would White Tobacco's crystal have told him that Rider was in trouble if Rider was already dead? Beehunter didn't think so. He thought that the old man's powers would have told him, but they had only told him that Rider was in trouble, and that he was somewhere west. Beehunter rode on, anxious and worried but hopeful.

Lovely looked up Cornshucks as fast as he could and offered to pay him to ride with him out of town. "I'll need you to interpret for me with Beehunter," he said. "There might be trouble out there, though. If there's any shooting, you just stay back out of the way. Will you go?"

"I'll go along," said Cornshucks.

As they rode along on the road going west out of town, Lovely filled Cornshucks in on his mission. "That was Chunk Harlan I killed, all right," he said. "Rider was taking Harlan from Tahlequah to Muskogee. From what I found out there, Harlan had some partners—four of them. They must have waylaid Rider to rescue Harlan—somewhere on the road from Tahlequah to Muskogee. Then they cut across this way. They must have skirted town, because I couldn't find anyone who had seen any of them except Harlan. Anyhow, Harlan sold Rider's horse in Wagoner."

"You think they killed Rider?" Cornshucks asked.

"I don't know," Lovely said. "I hope not."

"So why are we riding out this way?" Cornshucks asked.

"I don't know that, either," Lovely said, his voice sounding almost angry. "We're following Beehunter. That's all the hell I know."

Beehunter followed the tracks onto a path that led into the woods. The path was just wide enough for one horse. He slowed his pace. He stopped for a while and listened. The only sounds he heard were of squirrels and birds and the leaves rustling in the slight breeze. He moved ahead slowly. Then he stopped again. He could smell the smoke of a fire, probably a fire in a cook stove. He dismounted and took both horses into the woods, lapping their reins around a small tree. He opened one of the saddlebag pouches, reached in, and pulled out a box of shells. He opened the box and took out the bullets, stuffing them in his pockets. He put the empty box back into the bag, then pulled the Warner out of its sheath. He walked cautiously back out onto the path.

He moved along as quietly as he could, and soon he could detect the odor of meat cooking. It was a cook stove, just as he had figured, and whoever was up there was fixing a meal. That was good. He thought he'd give them time to start eating. He moved in a little closer, staying on the edge of the path, almost brushing against the foliage that grew thick there. He saw the cabin and the four horses tied to a rail in front. Four men. He moved in even closer now, then edged himself into the brush and under the trees. He watched.

Rider's inside there, he thought. I have to be careful. He eased himself through the tangled brush, slowly, making as little noise as possible. He found a spot from which he could watch, and shoot if necessary, and he settled in to wait. He didn't know just what he was waiting for, but he knew he could not realistically rush four men inside a cabin by himself, especially not with Rider in there.

It wasn't long before a man came out of the door to relieve himself. Beehunter was disgusted. That man hadn't gone three steps away from the door. Even before he had finished his business, the man turned his head to shout back toward the door. "You about got that meat cooked?" he said. "I should have left for Wagoner already. Chunk's going to be pissed off. He's waiting for me."

A voice came back from inside the cabin. "It's done now. Come and get it."

Beehunter watched as the man finished his chore and went back inside. The four men should be busy eating now, and he thought that he could move in on them and take them by surprise. It would still be risky, though. He waited, wondering what he should do. In a few minutes, the man who had come outside to pee came back out, holding a piece of meat wrapped in bread. He walked to one of the horses and mounted up. Beehunter hurried back through the woods a ways farther from the cabin. Here was a chance to narrow the odds.

As the man rode along the narrow pathway through the woods, gnawing on the meat and bread in his hand, Beehunter came out of the woods on the back of his roan. He swung the Warner hard, smashing its butt against the other man's neck. Beehunter calmed both horses as quickly as he could and moved them back into the brush. He dismounted, slid the man's limp body down off his horse, and tied him to a tree. Then he worked his way back through the woods.

He decided to move on in. He made it all the way to the cabin door without calling any attention to himself. He leaned the Warner against the side of the cabin. It would do him no good inside. Then he pulled out the Smith & Wesson. He stepped back, took a deep breath, then burst through the door. The three men at the table all started to jump up, with surprised looks on their faces. Beehunter fired, and one man fell, a dark splotch on his chest. The other two stopped still and raised their hands. "Don't shoot, mister," one of them said.

On a cot against the wall, Go-Ahead Rider slowly raised himself up. Beehunter could see that the side of Rider's head was covered in matted blood. "You all right, Go-Ahead?" he asked in Cherokee.

"I am now," Rider answered. "Just keep those two covered."

Rider got up slowly and made his way with unsteady steps over to the table. He took the guns from the holsters of the two men, then bent down to take one out of the waistband of the dead outlaw. He tossed two of the guns over to the cot and held the third one on the two prisoners. "I got them now," he said to Beehunter in Cherokee. "Tie them up."

As Rider and Beehunter were loading their prisoners onto the horses there at the cabin, Lovely and Cornshucks rode up. "Rider," Lovely said, "are you all right?"

"I will be," Rider said. "Thanks to Beehunter."

"What happened?"

"This bunch jumped me on the road to Muskogee," Rider said. "They took me along with them as a hostage just until they could meet with a big customer of theirs to get paid. Then I guess they meant to kill me and get out of the territory. The money man's in Wagoner. I know who he is. We can pick him up there."

"I'm sure relieved to find you in one piece," Lovely said. "Beehunter did a hell of a job. I just wish he could talk English."

Rider looked at Beehunter and grinned. "Aw," he said, "Beehunter don't need no English."

Bad Whiskey

Go-Ahead Rider was worried about Beehunter. Beehunter was totally reliable. He was not at all like what people thought about full-blood Indians, late all the time, undependable, going on "Indian time." Of course, Rider did not believe all that anyway. He himself was a full-blood Cherokee. But he knew what people said, even mixed-blood Cherokees. Be that as it may, Beehunter was usually at the office before Rider, and here he was an hour late. Rider kept telling himself that Beehunter had a good reason, and that everything was just fine. Even so, he worried.

As high sheriff of the Cherokee Nation in 1873, the year the railroad was coming through, Rider had plenty to worry about. The railroad would be bringing all kinds of people into the Cherokee Nation, most of them people that Rider and most full-blood Cherokees would rather do without. New towns would spring up almost overnight along the tracks. Already Cherokees were arguing with one another. It was mostly mixed-bloods who approved of the railroads and full-bloods who were against it. Chief John Ross had fought hard for years to keep the railroad out, but at the end of the Civil War, he had been forced to sign a new treaty, and the railroad was coming.

Strange white people were already showing up in Tahlequah every day, some wearing six-guns strapped to their hips, and Rider had to inform them that it was against the law to wear guns on the city streets. Beehunter mostly left the white people alone. He could not speak English. Where was Beehunter, Rider wondered. He tried to put the worry out of his mind by filling out some papers that he needed to have ready for the next council meeting, but the meeting was nearly a month away, and he had plenty of time. He decided to spend some time walking around town. He was near the north end of the main street when he saw Beehunter coming, walking across the log footbridge that stretched across Wolf Creek.

"Beehunter," Rider called out, speaking Cherokee, "what's happened to your horse?"

Beehunter did not answer immediately. He walked on over to Rider and held out his hand. Rider took it in his. "What happened?" he repeated.

"My horse fell," said Beehunter. "And then he ran away. I tried to catch him, but he ran too far, and I lost him. I had to walk on in."

"Come on, let's go to the office," Rider said.

They walked to the office, and Rider poured them each a cup of coffee. He sat behind his desk and looked at Beehunter. "What made your horse fall?" he asked.

Beehunter shrugged. "*Hla yagwanta*," he said. "I don't know. He just fell. There didn't seem to be any reason. I've had some bad luck lately. I think someone is making medicine against me."

"What are you going to do?"

"I need to go see George Panther."

Rider knew George Panther. In fact, he had gone to Panther himself on more than one occasion. Panther was one of the most respected Indian doctors, or medicine men, in the entire Cherokee Nation.

"We'll get you a horse out of the sheriff's barn," Rider said. "You can take the rest of the day to deal with this problem. When you're done at George's place, you can ride the horse home."

"You don't need me today?"

"I'll make out," Rider said.

As Beehunter rode toward George Panther's house, he thought of his neighbor down the road. Charlie Killer was a lazy, worthless man. His wife had taken the children and left him a couple of years earlier. Beehunter had caught him with some illegal whiskey one time and arrested him, and Charlie had hated Beehunter ever since that time. He never did tell Beehunter or Go-Ahead Rider who had sold him the whiskey. Whenever Beehunter happened to pass Charlie on the road, Charlie glared at him and did not speak. Beehunter suspected that Charlie had gone to see some unscrupulous doctor to work bad medicine on him.

Rider was seated at his desk again when Delbert Swim, another of his deputies, came into the office. Delbert could speak Cherokee and English, but for some reason he seemed to prefer speaking in English. Rider looked up when Swim walked in. "What's up, Delbert?" he asked.

"Go-Ahead," said Swim, "we got a problem."

"What is it?"

"There's a white man out there wearing a six-gun. I told him there's a law against it in Tahlequah, but he told me to go to hell."

Rider got up from behind his desk. "Show him to me," he said. Delbert Swim was not afraid of the white man. Rider knew that. It was just that the Cherokee authorities were not allowed by U.S. law to arrest or try white people for crimes committed in the Indian Territory. That included all the lands of the Cherokee, Creek, Choctaw, Chickasaw, and Seminole Nations. Unless there was a deputy U.S. marshal somewhere nearby, white men were allowed to run roughshod over Indians. And the real trouble was that most of the white people knew that and took advantage of it.

They walked the block down to the main street and turned to their right. In another block, Delbert Swim said, "There he is." He nodded toward the other side of the street, and Rider saw the man. A big redhead wearing black slacks, a dirty white shirt, and a black vest, he had a tall white hat on his head and a gun belt strapped around his middle.

"Go tell him again," Rider said.

"But he'll just—"

"Tell him."

Swim walked across the street and approached the man. The man recognized him at once and snarled. "Mister," said Swim, "I've been to see the sheriff, and he says—"

"I don't give a damn what he says," the redhead snapped. "How many times I got to tell you? I'm a white man. Your laws don't apply to me."

"Look," said Swim, "I don't want any trouble with you."

"Then leave me alone."

The man suddenly stiffened. He felt the barrel of Rider's .38 caliber Navy Colt poking into the small of his back. Rider reached with his left hand and took the revolver out of the man's holster. "Hey," said the man. "What is this?"

"I think you've been told," said Rider.

"You can't do this to me. I'm a white man."

"You can pick this thing up at my office when you're ready to leave town," Rider said.

Tony Smith was a half-breed who farmed southeast of Tahlequah. He was driving his wagon into town to pick up some supplies. A few miles out, he stopped the wagon to look off to his left, where he saw a coyote snuffling around on the ground. It was probably nothing, a dead calf or something, but he decided to take a closer look. He took the rifle from beneath the wagon seat and snapped off a shot to scare the coyote away. Then, taking the rifle with him, he walked out in the field. He had not gone far when he saw the body of a man.

"I think it's Charlie Killer," Beehunter was saying. He was seated beneath the arbor just outside the home of George Panther. Panther smiled and nodded his head slowly.

"Wait here," he said in Cherokee. "I'll be back."

Panther heaved his huge bulk up from the chair and turned to walk into his house. Beehunter knew that he was going inside to do what he called "reading on the problem." He might stare into his crystal, or he might do something else. Beehunter did not know and did not want to know. It was dangerous business. Leave it to George. But somehow, when George came back out of the house, he would know who was doing this to Beehunter, he would know why, and he would know what to do about it. Beehunter had absolute faith in that.

While he waited, George's wife, Gwed', came out of the house with a cup of coffee. She walked over to Beehunter and handed him the cup.

"*Wado*, Gwed'," Beehunter said.

"*Howa.*"

Smith pulled his wagon up in front of the rock building that housed the Cherokee National Prison and the office of the high sheriff of the Cherokee Nation. He set the brake and climbed down. Walking inside, he found Go-Ahead Rider sitting behind his desk. Rider looked up.

"Sheriff Rider?" said Smith.

"That's me. What can I do for you?"

"Come outside with me," Smith said.

Rider followed the farmer outside and down to the wagon. He saw the body even before Smith said anything, and he recognized it as that of John Jones, a white man and a deputy United States marshal. He could see that Jones had been shot one time in the chest.

"Where'd you find him?"

"About five miles out southeast of town. He was laying out in the field."

"Will you take me out there? I'll get you a riding horse out of the sheriff's barn."

George Panther gave Beehunter a bag of tobacco to smoke while walking a circle around his house. He gave him another bag to smoke in the direction of Charlie Killer's place. "This first one'll protect your house, your family, from what he's doing," Panther said. "This other one here will send it straight back to him. Whatever he's trying to do to you, it'll happen to him. And I found your horse. You know that place where he fell? Go back to that same place and walk toward the creek. You'll find him down there by the creek. I saw him real clear."

Beehunter nodded solemnly.

"And it is Charlie Killer," Panther said. "The reason he's doing it is that he was jealous of you all along, but then you arrested him that time, and he wants to get even. That's what it's all about."

It did not take Smith long to locate the spot where he had found the body. Rider could see a spot of blood there on the ground. He looked carefully. He could tell that a wagon had been through there.

"Did you drive your wagon out here to pick up the body?" he asked.

"No, I left it parked there in the road."

The wagon tracks went back out to the road, but from there they were of no use. Too many wagons had gone up and down there. Rider could find no other evidence at the scene of the crime. In fact, he wasn't even sure it was the scene of the crime. The marshal could have been killed elsewhere and his body brought to this spot in the wagon and then dumped. He rode back to town and thanked Smith for his help. The farmer got in his wagon and drove off to take care of business.

Rider took the horses back to the barn. Then he walked to the undertaker's parlor where he'd had the body taken. He studied it, not knowing what he was looking for. He suddenly realized that there was no badge showing. He turned out the vest. Still no badge. He called the undertaker over. "Melvin," he said, "have you taken anything off this body?"

"I ain't touched it, sheriff."

Rider felt the pockets. There was no blindfold. And Jones was not wearing a gun. Jones had been robbed. That was something to go on.

It was still a long shot, but if any of those things could be found, they would find the murderer. There were blank whiskey warrants in the vest pocket, but the deputy marshals always carried those. Whiskey was illegal in the Indian Territory.

He got back to his office just in time to meet the redhead. "I came for my gun," the man said.

"You leaving town?" asked Rider.

"And none too soon," the man said.

Rider noticed another wagon parked in front of the prison, its bed covered by a canvas tarp. "That yours?" he asked.

"Yeah. What of it?"

Rider walked into his office ahead of the man and handed him the revolver. The redhead stuck it in his holster and stomped out of the room. Rider moved to the window and watched the man drive away. Something told him to follow.

Riding the horse that Rider had loaned him, Beehunter moved toward the creek where George Panther had told him he would find his own horse. He rode just into the trees that lined the creek, dismounted, and tied the horse. It would be easier to catch his own on foot. He was about to move on down to the creek when he heard the sound of a wagon approaching. He stopped, hidden by the trees, and watched as a redheaded man drove his wagon off the road, down through the trees, and stopped at a spot near the creek. Just watering his horse, he thought. He went on down the creek himself and found his horse. It was still saddled, and it was no trouble at all to catch. He could not see down the creek to where the redheaded man was. Back where the borrowed horse waited, he was about to mount up when he saw Charlie Killer coming on his mule. He decided to keep hidden a little longer.

Rider moved down the road slowly. He did not want the man to know he was being followed. He was surprised when he saw Beehunter step out of the woods and motion for him. He rode his horse over to where Beehunter waited and dismounted.

"What's up?" he asked.

"Charlie Killer just met a white man in a wagon," Beehunter said. "They're right down there."

Charlie Killer tipped back a jug for a long swallow. At last he stopped to take a breath.

"You want some more, Charlie?" the man asked. "I won't be back in these parts for a while."

"I'll take one more," Killer said.

The man walked over to his wagon and lifted the tarp that covered its contents. He was reaching for another jug. Charlie suddenly grimaced. He dropped the jug and clutched at his stomach. He doubled over. "Ahh," he groaned. He drew a knife out from under his jacket, forced himself to stand up straight, stepped forward, and drove the knife into the man's back. As Rider and Beehunter stepped out of the woods, Charlie Killer fell back dead. They saw the knife in the white man, but they could see no cause of death for Charlie Killer.

"What happened?" Beehunter asked.

Rider looked at Killer's distorted features. "Poison whiskey," he said. He knelt beside the dead white man to check his pockets, and he found Jones's billfold and badge. He looked up at Beehunter. "We'd better get these bodies into town," he said, "and then notify the U.S. marshals."

Aunt Jenny

Nobody remembered when they took to calling her Aunt Jenny; nor
were they quite sure why. Maybe it was because "Widow Jenny" had
never seemed quite right, and maybe "Mamaw Jenny" seemed somehow
disrespectful. She was sitting in a rocking chair on the small porch of
her log cabin near Cherokee, Alabama, when the wagon pulled up carrying a coffin. Some men climbed down from the wagon and unloaded
the coffin, carrying it to the porch. The old woman did not even look at
them. She had already received word that it was on its way. As the men
stepped down off the porch, one of them tipped his hat to her and said,
"Sorry, Aunt Jenny." She did not respond.

Another man who had been in the wagon came up onto the porch
carrying a pad and a pencil. He stopped in front of her and hesitated.
"Aunt Jenny," he said.

"I don't know you," she said, "and I ain't your aunt."

"I beg your pardon, Mrs. Brooks," he said. "Everyone calls you that.
I'm Borden Larson from the *Birmingham Gazette*. I'm sure it's small
comfort to you, but this is big news. Henry was, I believe, the last of your
sons. I wonder if you have any comment to make."

"They all died with their boots on," she said. "And he was my grandson. My baby."

"Mrs. Brooks," said Larson, "may I ask—how old are you?"

"I'm eighty-one years old, and I've outlived 'em all."

"How many children did you have?"

"I had four, three boys and a daughter," she said. "Sit down if you're
goin' to keep blatherin' at me."

Larson pulled a chair over close to Aunt Jenny and sat down. He
scribbled a few notes on his pad.

"Four," she went on. "All mine and Willis's. Willis has been gone now
for near fifty years. And now all his sons and grandsons is gone, too."

"Mrs. Brooks," Larson said, "if you don't mind my asking you—how did all the violence in your family get started?"

"It all come about," she said, "when Willis got hisself killed. The Civil War was ragin' then. It was eighteen and sixty-three. It was springtime. Willis had been away fightin' with the Confederates. He never had no use for Yankees. Tories we called 'em, you know. Well, he hadn't hardly been home before some of them Tory rascals come ridin' up to the house. They was seven of 'em. The one in charge was named Spears. I knowed him on account of all the while Willis had been gone, Spears had been comin' around to the house pesterin' me and my daughter. We knowed what it was he was wantin', but we never give in. Willis went out on the porch, right over there, and I follered him. He was totin' his six-gun. I seen Spears, and I said to Willis, 'That there is the bastard what's been after me and Frances.'

"Willis got a mean look on his face then, and he hollered out, 'What do you want here?'

"'We're lookin' for Johnny Rebs,' ole Spears called out, 'and we heared that you was one.' Willis cocked his gun and raised it up, but before he could pull the trigger, all seven of them bastards commenced to shootin'. I knowed 'em all. Each and every one of 'em. I thought Willis never would fall down, but he eventually did." She paused and pointed to a spot on the porch off to her left. "Right there he did. Fell down dead. 'Let's kill her, too,' one of the men said, but Spears stopped 'em. 'We ain't makin' war on women,' he said. 'Bring him along.' Two of the men dismounted and come up onto the porch. They picked up what was left of Willis and throwed him over one of their horses, and then the bunch of 'em rode off. They left me standin' there on the porch all by my lonesome. I never cried a tear, though. I was mad."

"I bet you were," said Larson. "What did you do?"

"I run into the house and got Willis's long gun. I checked it real quick to make sure it was loaded and ready to fire, and then I hurried back out onto the porch, but they was done out of sight. About three days later, I noticed that my oldest boy, John, didn't come home. After a coupla more days, I begun to worry. Then, finally, someone come to the house in a wagon, and they was bringin' both bodies to me, Willis and John. John had been shot up, too. Both bodies was found tossed into sinkholes. I prepared 'em both for buryin'. Then I called my other boys together—Mack and Willis Jr. I gethered 'em around me right here on the porch. I was settin' in this same chair. I put my hands on their heads, and I said, 'Boys, them lowdown Tory bastards has kilt your paw and your big brother. They never give 'em a chance. I know who they was, and I've writ down all their names for you right here on this paper,' and I handed the paper to Mack on account of he was the oldest.

"He looked at it, and Willis Jr. craned his neck to see it, too. 'You know 'em all,' I said. 'Now I want you two to make me a promise and swear to it right here and now that won't neither of you rest till all seven of these damn Tories is dead and buried. You understand me?'

"'Yes, Mama,' they said.

"'Now, swear it,' I said. And they did. Both of 'em. They swore that solemn oath. That was in eighteen and sixty-three."

1867

Mack came running into the house out of breath. He nearly fell down when he stopped running. He leaned both hands on the table where his mama was sitting husking corn. Willis Jr. was lying on the floor reading a book.

"Land sakes," said Jenny, "what has got into you?"

Mack was breathing heavily. "Mama," he said, panting, "I seen him. I seen Spears. He's come home from the army. But he's still wearin' that damn blue Tory uniform."

"Mack," she snapped back at him, "don't you be cussin' in this house. I've raised you better'n that."

"I'm sorry, Mama, but I just seen him in town."

Jenny's face grew stern, her eyes steely. "Well, then," she said, "you boys know what has to be done. You know where your daddy's guns is put away. Go fetch 'em out."

Mack crossed the room to where a large old trunk sat against the wall. Opening it, he lifted out the tray that sat on top and placed it aside on the floor. Then he turned over some linen that had been folded to cover everything else in the trunk, revealing two Remington New Model .44 caliber revolvers, each in a holster with a belt attached. He took them gingerly out of the trunk and carried them to the table. Jenny picked them up one at a time and inspected them. She found them fully loaded. That was no surprise, for she kept them that way. She hefted one and handed it to Mack. "Here," she said, "strap this on." She then held the other one out toward her youngest son. "Take this, Willis," she said, "and fetch the long gun down off the wall." Willis took the Remington without a word and strapped it on around his waist. Then he walked across to where the Colt model 1855 five-shot revolving rifle was hanging on the wall. He hefted it and brought it down. Jenny gestured to him to hand it to her. He did, and she inspected it for a full load, finding it ready.

"He'll be headin' right on to his old house," Mack said. "I heard him say so."

"Then don't be wastin' no time dilly-dallyin' around here," Jenny said. "Get on your way."

Mack reached the door first and pulled it open, but Jenny called out one more thing. "Mack," she said.

He hesitated and looked back at her. "Yes, Mama?"

"You carryin' your big knife?"

"Yes."

"Bring me his head."

The two boys stared a moment at their mother with grim looks on their faces. Then they ran out the door. Mack led the way.

When they reached the spot in the road that Mack had selected for their ambush, they were all out of breath, partly from running through the woods, partly from the excitement and anticipation of their imminent act. They hid themselves in the trees beside the road and waited tensely. "Mack," said Willis, in a voice barely above a whisper, "I ain't never kilt no one before."

"Well, hell," returned Mack, "me neither. You know that, don't you? What the hell difference does that make? There ain't nothin' to it, is there? You just point the gun and pull the trigger, that's all."

"You better not let Mama hear you cussin' like that," Willis said.

"Never you mind about that. She cusses aplenty anyhow."

"But she don't want us doin' it."

Mack was thinking about his father and his older brother who had been killed by this Spears nearly four years ago. He was thinking about all the time they had waited for this opportunity to fulfill their promise to their mother. He was thinking about blasting a hole in Spears's back and watching him die in the dirt. Then he heard the sounds of an approaching horse on the road, and he tensed.

In another moment, the horse and rider appeared. Mack and Willis stepped out into the road in front of Spears in an attempt to block his path. Spears reined in his mount, and Mack drew out his revolver. Willis pulled his out, too.

"Hello, Mr. Spears," Mack said.

"What the hell is this?" said Spears. "Ain't you the Brooks boys?"

"We are," said Mack, "and you murdered our paw."

"Now, wait a minute, boys," said Spears, his right hand easing toward his own revolver hanging at his side. "That was in wartime. The war is over now."

"That's no excuse, you rotten bastard," sneered Mack. He raised his gun, took quick aim, and fired. The bullet smacked Spears right in the throat. He jerked and howled, or tried to, though it sounded more like a whimper. Then Mack and Willis both cut loose with their handguns, hitting Spears with several shots into his chest. He jerked with each impact, and finally he slid sideways off his horse, his lifeless body smashing to the ground like a sack of flour. The boys ran to the body and stood staring down at their handiwork.

"Mack," said Willis, "you heard Mama. You got to cut off his head."

Mack drew out his long hunting knife and knelt beside the bloody body. "Go ahead, do it," said Willis, but he didn't feel much like watching.

Cutting deep, Mack sliced around the neck until he reached the bones. Then he started having difficulties. He couldn't cut through the bones. He kept slicing, and at the same time, he grabbed the head by the hair and twisted and jerked. At last he broke through, and the head came off in his hand. He wiped the knife blade on Spears's Union jacket.

Willis was nearly sick. "Let's get home," he said.

Mack checked the body and found a Starr .44 caliber single-action revolver, which he pulled out and stuck in his own waistband. "Good. Let's take his horse, too."

The two boys climbed on the back of the horse and headed it for their house, Mack still lugging his grisly trophy, leaving a trail of blood that anyone could follow. When they reached the house, they found their mother out in front with a fire going, and a bucket of water on the fire boiling. She looked up when the boys rode in. "That his horse you're ridin'?" she asked.

"Yes, Mama," said Mack, dropping down off the animal and heading toward the fire.

Then Willis Jr. swung down out of the saddle.

"Well," Jenny said, "take it around back out of sight and put it in the corral." She looked up as Willis started around the house with the horse, and then she saw Mack coming toward her toting the head, still holding it by its hair. "That's a good job, son," she said. Then, gesturing toward the boiling water, she added, "Just drop it in here." Mack did as he was told. Willis Jr. came back, and the boys stood around the fire with their mother watching the hated head boil.

Jenny and her boys sat around the table for breakfast the following morning eating a hearty meal of fried eggs, sausage, gravy, biscuits, and lots of coffee. The cleaned and polished skull sat on the table staring at them through its great hollow eye sockets. Jenny took a slug of coffee and said, "You boys are goin' to have to get out of here."

"What do you mean, Mama?" asked Mack.

"What did you do with the body?"

"Well, we just left it lay there where we kilt him."

"It won't be long 'fore they find it," she said. "And you left a drippin' blood trail right to the house. We got his horse. They'll be after you sure enough, and likely right soon, too."

"They can't prove that we done it, Mama," Mack said.

"I reckon they can prove it enough to suit their purposes," Jenny said. "I want you to get your stuff packed up and clear out of here soon as you finish your meal. Take our horse, and take his, too. I'd say ride west, and when you get to someplace where you want to set a spell, write me a letter. I'll let you know when any of the rest of 'em is back in these parts."

Soon Mack and Willis Jr. were riding away from their house, heading west, but they had not gone far when Mack said, "Say, ole Johnson's place is right on our way. Why don't we swing by there and see if he come home, too?"

"He mighta," said Willis.

"All right," said Mack. "We'll make a quick check when we ride by."

In a few more minutes they were there. They stopped on a rise sitting in the road on their horses, Mack on the family nag and Willis mounted on what had been Spears's horse.

"I can't tell nothin' from here," said Mack.

"That's a fresh horse in his corral, ain't it?" said Willis.

"I never seen it before," Mack said.

"Look, hangin' out on the line," said Willis. "I see a blue coat."

"By god, you're right," said Mack. "Let's go get him."

Johnson heard a knock at his door and went to answer it. When he opened the door, he saw the Brooks boys standing there with pistols in their hands. He opened his mouth as if to speak, but bullets from their two guns stopped him. He fell back into his house, blood pouring from his chest, and thudded on the floor. The boys whooped and ran back to their horses, mounting up and heading west as fast as they could manage.

"We got two of 'em," Mack shouted. "Two of 'em!"

"That still leaves five," said Willis.

They rode hard, probably too hard for the horses, but just before they reached the Mississippi line, they spotted a campfire. They rode slowly up on it. It was a small fire, and one man sat at it boiling some coffee. His horse, still saddled, stood quietly nearby. "We could sure use that horse," said Mack.

"You talkin' about stealin' it?" said Willis, incredulous.

"Hell," said Mack, "we done kilt two men. What's stealin' a horse?"

"We shoulda stole Johnson's horse back when we kilt him," Willis said.

"Well, we never. We was too anxious to get outta there," Mack said.

"Well, let's go get this one, then, if you say so," said Willis.

They rode easy into the camp, and the stranger welcomed them. He was a nice enough fellow, pleasant and easygoing. After drinking some of his coffee and making friendly small talk, Mack pulled out his Remington and leveled it at the man.

"Hey," the man said, "what is this?"

"It's a holdup, mister," said Willis. "We're takin' your horse."

"And your money," Mack added.

They left the man sitting alone drinking his coffee and lamenting the loss of his horse and his money and his guns and ammunition. The boys crossed into Mississippi. They had not gone far before they came to a small settlement. They stopped at a store there and bought some groceries. They used up most of the money they had stolen from the man in Alabama. They rode on out of town, still moving west. They were thinking about stopping and making a camp for the night and fixing something to eat when they came across an abandoned cabin. After checking it over, they decided to spend the night there.

It was comfortable enough, and they built a fire and prepared a meal. After they were satisfied, they rolled out their blankets and settled in for the night. In the morning, they rose up and fixed some breakfast.

"We just as well get started," Mack said.

"Where we goin'?" asked Willis.

"Mama just said for us to head west," Mack said.

"She never said how far west," said Willis. "We done went west. We got out of Alabama. This place ain't bad. And there's a town real close where we can mail a letter and tell her where she can write to us."

"I don't know," said Mack.

"Where we goin' to find us another house?" said Willis. "I say we stick right here. That way when we hear from Mama that another one of them Tories is back home, we won't have too far to ride to get him."

So it was decided. They would stay put in this abandoned house in Mississippi. They went back into town and sent a letter to their mother telling her where they could be reached, general delivery. Then they put out the word that they were looking for work, and they began to do odd jobs around town and the countryside surrounding it. Every few days they would check at the post office to see if they had any mail. The time dragged on for them. They had been in Mississippi about three weeks when they at last received a letter. It said only, "Lane and Bradford is come home. Mama."

The boys loaded up their weapons and packed lightly. They mounted up and headed for home. They knew where Lane had lived back in '63, but they had no idea about Bradford, so they rode straight for their own old home. Mama cooked them a good meal, and they ate it with relish, while Spears's skull watched over them, grinning. They had not eaten this well since they left home. Then they told her that they did not know where to find Bradford.

"You know where Lane's place is?" she said. "It's right where it always was."

"We know it," Mack said.

"Just keep on goin' down the road from there. Bradford's is the next place."

"We'll get 'em, Mama," said Mack.

"Ain't no time like the present," said Willis.

"You boys got plenty of bullets?" she asked them.

"Yes, Mama," said Mack. "We're all set."

"Well, be careful. I love you both."

The boys hugged and kissed their mama and then rode out again. They headed for the old Lane place. It was not far. They planned to stop at Lane's, kill him, then ride on to Bradford's. They would kill Bradford and then head back west, back to their new home, the abandoned cabin in Mississippi.

When they reached Lane's place, they found him in the yard splitting wood. He did not pay much attention as the two riders approached. When they drew near, he sank his ax in a log and looked up, wiping his brow on a sleeve. "Howdy," he said. "What can I do for you?" Then he wrinkled his brow. "Say, ain't you—"

Mack shot him first, his bullet tearing through Lane's throat from front to back. Then Willis shot him in the chest, and Mack sent another slug into his chest. Lane fell down on a stack of unsplit logs, and Willis and Mack each shot him three more times in the back. "Let's get goin'," said Willis, and he whipped up his horse and headed back toward the road. Mack followed him, and they rode fast on down the road toward where their mother had said they would find Bradford.

Bradford was inside his house when he heard the horses riding into the yard. He went to a window and looked out, and he recognized the Brooks brothers. He knew what he had done to their father and brother, and he figured out what they were doing at his house. He grabbed a rifle and headed out the back door. Hills rose sharply behind his house, and he ran for them. Mack had gotten off his horse and was on the porch when he heard the back door slam. "He's run out the back," he yelled to Willis. He started running to his left around the house. Willis dismounted quickly and ran around the house to the right. They reached the back corners of the house at the same time. They looked toward the hills and saw Bradford running and looking over his shoulder. He saw them and turned, firing a wild shot.

Mack returned fire, a quick shot that tore the heel of Bradford's right foot. Bradford fell down screaming in pain. He scrambled to a nearby large rock for cover. Getting behind the boulder, he leveled his rifle and fired again, this time just missing Willis. Willis shot back, his bullet nicking the boulder and sending shards of rock over Bradford's head. Bradford hunkered down.

The brothers started running, Mack staying to the left of the big rock, Willis moving to its right. Bradford looked up to see the movement and fired a shot in Mack's direction, but when he did, Willis shot at him from the other side. Bradford turned to defend that side, but by that time Mack had moved closer and had a clear shot at him. Willis raised his pistol and fired a well-placed shot that broke Bradford's left shoulder. As Bradford tried to operate his rifle with just his right hand, Mack snapped off a shot that caught him in the chest. He slumped behind the rock.

The boys moved in slowly, watching closely for any movement from their victim. When they were right on top of him, Mack reached out with a foot and shoved, and the body rolled over. They could see that he was dead. Mack picked up the rifle, and they left. As they mounted their horses to ride on, Willis said, "We've got four of 'em."

"There's still three more," said Mack.

1868

Jenny Brooks was alone in her house. She was chopping cabbage for her supper. She was alone because her daughter, Frances, had married Sam Baker that spring and moved out of the house. Her two surviving boys, Mack and Willis Jr., were living in Mississippi, to stay away from the Colbert County, Alabama, law. Jenny was paying a high price for her revenge, but it was worth it, she thought. She looked at the skull on her table and smiled.

She was about thirty-nine years old, but she looked older. Her life had not been an easy one. She did not even know for sure what her age was. She approximated it when she was asked or when she thought about it. She did not know who her parents were or where or when she had been born. Her earliest memories were vague. There was a house and a garden, pigs and cows and horses. There must have been parents, but she had no memory of them. She thought the house was in North Carolina, but she couldn't be sure of that.

She did have a clear and distinct memory of soldiers barging into the house one day and dragging them all outside, then marching them a long way down the hills until they came to a stockade prison where it seemed that hundreds of Cherokees were being held. She did not understand it at the time. She learned later. They were being held until the army was ready to march them west over what would become known as the Trail of Tears. The year was 1838. She must have been around nine years old. She should have a better memory of the times, she thought. Perhaps her mind had blocked it out. It had been too horrible a time. She did remember when the army had let them out of the stockade and started moving them west. She remembered thinking that they would walk forever.

She remembered being miserably tired from walking, from falling down and getting up to continue walking. She had no memory of what had become of her parents. Perhaps they had died, or perhaps they had been killed. Perhaps they had even managed to run away. If so, they ran away and left her alone on the trail. She had no feelings for them.

Then she recalled the day when they had stopped at a farmhouse. The people there, unlike most of the white people they met along the way, were kindhearted, and when the Cherokees and the soldiers resumed their march, Jenny was left behind. If she had ever known why, she couldn't remember. She was an orphan. At least she thought that she had been. Maybe the farmers just offered to care for her, and no one else had any better solution. Maybe the soldiers had sold her to the farmer. It didn't matter. The farmers became her new family. They gave her a place to sleep and they fed her well, but she had to work for her keep.

The years went by, and then one day Willis Brooks stopped by the farm. He was invited to supper, and then to stay the night. She must have been about fifteen years old, she thought. Willis was thirty-six. She knew what he wanted by the way he looked at her. He bargained with her foster parents, and when he left the next day, Jenny left with him. She became his wife. Willis was a wanderer, and he had fought Mexico with Texas, and before that he had fought the Creek Indians with General Jackson. There were no wars to fight in 1844, though, and he settled on a piece of land in Colbert County, Alabama, that had been given to him for his service with Jackson.

They settled in to farm, and Jenny Brooks began having his children. The first was John, born in 1846. He was only seventeen years old when the damned Tories killed him. A year later, Mack came along. The next year brought Willis Jr. Finally came Frances in 1850.

Sometimes Jenny wondered if she was really Cherokee. When she looked at herself in a mirror, she did not think she appeared to be an Indian. Maybe she was a Cherokee breed. The times she almost really believed it were when she looked at Mack. He did appear to be Indian. She thought of him as her Cherokee boy. Sometimes she wished that she knew for sure. Who were her parents? And what were they?

But now her husband was dead, and so was her firstborn son. Her daughter was married and away from home, and her two remaining sons were fugitives. But they were doing good work. They were avenging the deaths of Willis and John. In a way, a perverse way, they might even be avenging the loss of her parents. They might be avenging the whole damned Trail of Tears. Jenny looked at the skull on the table and reached out with her knife to rap on the top of the hollow head. She smiled at it as she did so.

Sheriff Alex Heflin stood on the board sidewalk in front of his office in Cherokee, Alabama. A crowd was gathered in the street in front of him.

"It's them damn Brooks brothers," one of the men said. "We all know it."

"That's right, Alex," said another. "When Spears and them other men killed old Willis and maybe his boy John, the brothers went after them for revenge."

"Everyone knows it," said yet another. "They was seven men kilt Willis, and the men that's been murdered around here lately was all part of them seven."

"All right, all right," said Heflin. "I'll go after the Brooks brothers and bring 'em in for trial."

"They don't need no trial," said a man in the crowd. "They just needs to be kilt."

"If you can catch 'em without killin' 'em, then you oughta just hang 'em right then."

"Now, there won't be none of that," Heflin said. "Come on, now. Let's cut out all this jabberin' and get a posse together."

In Mississippi, the brothers had just received word from home that another of the original seven on their list had returned to northwest Alabama. They were getting ready to ride when they saw the posse coming. They jumped on their horses and lit out in the opposite direction, fleeing from the approaching lawmen. They had not ridden far when they turned off the road and went up the side of a steep hill. They dismounted and took cover, taking their rifles with them.

"Who the hell are they?" asked Mack.

"Damned if I know," said Willis.

"I think it's a posse from Cherokee," said Mack. "I could see Alex Heflin with 'em."

"But that ain't legal," Willis said. "They're plumb outta Alabama."

"They don't care about legal," Mack said. "They just want us. Here they come."

The boys opened fire with their rifles, dropping three posse men at once. The others hauled in their mounts. Some began returning fire, but they had not spotted their targets and were shooting wild.

"Get down and take cover," Heflin shouted.

While the lawmen were dismounting, the boys hit three more, so half the posse was out of commission. The rest were all scampering for cover. "Let's ride outta here," said Willis. He and Mack got back to their mounts and headed on over the mountain. Soon they were on another road on the other side.

"Where we goin'?" Mack asked.

"Let's go back home to Mama's house," Willis said. "It'd be safer there."

They abandoned all of their belongings in the cabin in Mississippi and headed back for Cherokee, Alabama. When they reached a hilltop outside of Cherokee, they sat on their horses and looked down on the town.

"If we ride down and take a back street, we might can go through town without no one seein' us," Mack said.

"Be even safer if we was to ride plumb around the town," said Willis.

"It'll take quite a bit longer," Mack said. "Why don't we just ride straight through on Main Street and hoo-raw the town on our way through?"

"That would show 'em what we think about their damned illegal posse comin' after us in Mississippi," said Willis with a grin on his face. "Let's do it."

They pulled out their pistols and held them up in front of their faces. Then they gave each other a look and kicked their horses in the sides. As they rode into Cherokee, they were whooping and shooting into the air. Mack fired a couple of shots into store windows. People were running and shouting, diving into stores or behind water troughs or barrels for cover. Women screamed for their children.

"Someone get the sheriff!"

"He's out chasin' the Brooks brothers."

"This right here is the Brookses!"

"God damn it."

There was no one to be seen on the street, no voice to be heard, as the brothers rode out the other end of town.

A frustrated Sheriff Heflin led his posse back toward Alabama. He couldn't figure out how the Brooks brothers had managed to escape from him. He knew he had been right behind them.

"Maybe they crossed over that mountain back there, Alex," said Rance Stoddard. Rance was particularly interested in capturing or killing the brothers, as he was one of the original seven men who had killed Willis Sr. and John. "Maybe we should have crossed over it ourselves."

"It woulda been a waste of time," said Heflin. "We didn't see no tracks, did we? We couldn't know for sure that was the way they went."

"But it makes sense," said Stoddard. "They could—"

"Just shut up about it, Rance," Heflin said. "We're way out of our jurisdiction anyhow."

It was around noon the next day when they got back to Cherokee, and they had no sooner shown themselves than people came running out of stores.

"Sheriff," one man said, "the Brooks brothers was here."

"They shot up the town," said another.

"Rode in shootin' and rode right out again."

"Headin' that-a-way."

"We got to get after them," said Stoddard.

"Come on," said Heflin, and he led the way through town. "They're headed for their mama's place."

Everyone in the posse knew where Jenny Brooks lived. They headed straight for it. Their mounts were tired, but they pushed them on. They would have been smarter to get fresh horses before continuing, but they were agitated and frustrated. Sheriff Heflin was mad that the boys had eluded him, and Stoddard was fearful for his own life unless they were caught and killed soon.

Jenny was surprised to see her sons come riding up to the house. She met them on the porch. "What are you doin' back here?" she asked. "Don't you know that the sheriff is after you?"

"Take it easy, Maw," said Mack. "We left him back in Mississippi."

"Chasin' a wild goose," said Willis. "You got somethin' to eat, Mama?" he added, stepping up onto the porch to hug Jenny.

She gave him a warm embrace and said, "Course I do. Come on in, boys."

They were soon seated around the table, looking at the skull while Jenny laid out bread and cold roast beef. The boys attacked it with relish. "Mama," said Mack, "you're the best cook I've ever knowed." Jenny poured coffee all around. They had eaten their fill when they heard the horses approaching outside. Mack ran to a window to look out. "It's Heflin and that damned posse," he said.

"Our rifles are out with the horses," said Willis, and he ran to the door, jerked it open, and ran out. Grabbing the rifles, he made it back through the door as bullets smashed into the house around him. Mack slammed the door shut. Willis handed a rifle to Mack, who opened the door again, but only a crack. He poked the rifle barrel through the small opening and fired. Willis fired through the front window. One posse member had dismounted and was running to his left in an attempt to get around to the side of the house. Willis dropped him with a shot to the leg.

Mack said, "Hey, do you recognize that guy out there with the green jacket on?"

"Yeah," Willis answered. "That's Rance Stoddard. Kill the bastard." They both fired their rifles at Stoddard, who fell to the ground, hit by at least four bullets. Then there was another shot. It came from behind the posse, and another of the lawmen dropped from his horse. The posse men all turned to face their rear, and as they did, Mack shot one in the back. Shots were suddenly flying wild. Heflin shouted for everyone to mount up and get out of there, and they did. The shots slowed down some as the posse retreated. Heflin, on his own horse, led a horse over to where the man with the leg wound still lay on the ground. He helped the man into the saddle, and they both rode off.

The immediate danger past, the boys and their mother all stepped out onto the porch. They looked over the scene of carnage. In another minute, a buggy came driving into the yard. "It's your sister and her husband," said Jenny.

"Sam," said Mack, "was that you doin' that shootin' back there?"

"Hell," said Sam Baker, stepping down out of the buggy, "I couldn't let you have all the fun, could I?"

"Did any of 'em see you?" asked Willis.

"Aw, I think ole Heflin got a look at me as he rode off," said Sam. "I thought about shootin' him, but it seemed like the fight was done over with."

"Maybe you shoulda kilt him anyhow," said Mack. "If he recognized you, you'll be wanted now, too."

"I ain't goin' to let that worry me none," Sam said. "Hell, from now on, I'm with you boys. Willis Sr. was my wife's daddy, too. And John was her big brother."

So now they were three. Mack was all for heading back to Mississippi for safety, but Willis pointed out that the posse had followed them to Mississippi and knew the location of their hideout there. "That's right," said Mack. "We're just as safe right here at home."

"We can't stay here, though," said Willis. "Mama'd be in danger if they come back here lookin' for us. We got to find another place to stay."

Frances looked up into her husband's eyes. "Sam," she said, "couldn't they stay at our place?"

"Why, sure," said Sam.

"I don't know about that, neither," said Willis.

"What's wrong with it?" said Sam.

"It'd be puttin' our sister in danger," Willis told him, "and I don't—"

"I can shoot a gun," said Frances.

"Besides that," Sam added, "we'll post lookouts. Then we'll know if anyone's comin'. We can get ready for them or we can get away. It's all settled."

Mack looked at Willis. "What do you think?" he asked.

"Let's go look at their place and then decide," said Willis.

They found the Baker place almost ideal. The house and barn were built on a flat piece of land but were surrounded by steep mountains. One narrow lane led into the tiny valley. Sam Baker pointed out a horse trail that led up the steep mountain behind the house. He also pointed out a spot on a mountainside in front of the house and to the right where a fine place could be fixed up for a guard. From there a man could see well down the narrow road that led up to the house. Then they looked over the barn and found that it was built at least as well as the house. It could be fitted out for three men to sleep in easily. Mack and Willis agreed that it would be a good place to stay. They were back close to their mama. They could see her regularly and eat her fine cooking. Frances could cook, too. She had learned from their mama, but Mama's cooking was still the best.

They were also right close for when the last two men on their list would show up again, but they knew that would not be the end of it. They knew that there would never be an end to it, for now they were wanted by the law, now they were fugitives. There might have been some sympathy for them for killing the men on their list, the ones who had killed their father and brother, but now they had also killed posse men. They were outlaws, and they had just as well get used to it. They could terrorize the countryside.

They could take over Colbert County and run it the way they wanted to. Why not? They had already driven off Alex Heflin and his posse. There had been nothing to it. They could do it again and again. It would not be long before everyone in Colbert County would know better than to mess with the Brooks brothers. Willis thought about Sam Baker. Maybe the Brooks gang would be a better designation now, he thought.

Mack sat in front of the Baker barn cleaning his Starr revolver. He had already cleaned and reloaded his rifle. It was leaning against the barn behind him. Willis was currying his horse. Inside the house, Frances was preparing the noon meal. She had made biscuits, had baked a ham, and was boiling corn and beans. She was stirring gravy on the stove. The coffee was ready, and it all smelled awfully good.

Outside, a young girl rode up to the house on a sorrel mare. She rode astride the saddle the way a man would, in spite of the fact that it was generally considered to be in bad taste for a woman to ride that way. The gal, who may have been around sixteen years old, was dressed like a boy. Her jeans fit her tight and revealed her fine figure. Her shirt was tied at the bottom and revealed a small amount of white skin above her jeans. She tossed her strawberry blond hair as she moved to the front door, letting her hat fall behind her head, where it was held by a string that had been under her chin but was now around her neck. She did not bother knocking but opened the door and walked right in.

Over at the barn door, Willis watched her with interest. He wondered who the good-looking and bold young girl might be. He finished currying the horse as quickly as he could, patted it, and then walked to the house. "Looks like we got company, Sis," he said.

The girl looked at him and smiled. Frances said, "Willis, this is my sister-in-law, Sam's sister Bedelia. You likely heard tell of her, but what with hidin' out in Mississippi and all, I guess you never did meet her. Bedelia, this here is my brother Willis."

Willis stepped forward and held out his right hand. Bedelia took it in hers and held it a moment, and the feel of her touch sent a thrill through his whole body. "I'm mighty glad to make your acquaintance, Miss Bedelia," he said.

"Thank you," she said. "I'm pleased to meet you. I've heard a passel of stuff about you."

"Was it good or bad?" he asked.

"I guess it all depends on who you are," she said. "I took it all good. You been killin' Yankee Tories is what I keep hearin' about."

"I reckon that much is true enough," he said.

"Power to you, Willis," she said.

"Willis," said Frances, "tell your brother to come on in to dinner."

"All right, Sis," he said. Tearing himself away from the mesmerizing gaze of Bedelia Baker, he walked to the door, opened it, and stepped outside. "Mack," he called out, "the food's ready. Get your lazy butt on over here."

When they had finished the meal, Willis got bold. He asked Bedelia if she would like to go for a walk, and she readily agreed. He thought about pointing out their horse trail escape route back behind the house, but something told him to keep that to himself. They walked around to the front of the house and a ways down the road. Then he took her for a hike up the mountainside to their lookout post. It was absolutely hidden from anywhere down below, but once they reached it, she saw that it was lined with a rock wall and had a rock perch behind the wall where a man with a rifle could sit and have a clear shot at any point down on the road. He also could see someone coming for a long ways and have plenty of time to get down and warn others at the house or the barn of the approach. At the back of the spot there was a depression in the mountainside, not quite deep enough to call a cave, but enough to back into to get out of the rain. Inside there were boxes of .45 shells. The Brooks gang was well established in this place.

Bedelia took it all in with admiration. She liked what these outlaws were doing. The Bakers were a Confederate family just like the Brookses. For years she had been hearing about what Spears and the others had done to Willis Brooks Sr. and to John. Then when she heard about what the brothers were doing, she was delighted. Finally, she had been thrilled to learn that her brother had joined with them. No, the war was not yet over to Bedelia Baker, any more than it seemed to be to the Brooks brothers. She was thrilled to be out walking with Willis Brooks. He was the youngest, but it was widely rumored that he was the closest to being the leader of the gang.

"Well," said Willis at last, "I reckon we oughta be gettin' on back down."

She put a hand on his shoulder, and he turned to look at her. Then she placed her other hand on his other shoulder and looked up into his face. There was no mistaking her look. Willis put his arms around her and pulled her to him. He lowered his face and kissed her on the lips. They lingered with the kiss. It was long and pleasurable and passionate. When at last they broke it up, they stood staring into each other's eyes. Then they kissed again.

Back in the Baker house, Willis made sure that everyone was there. "Everyone sit down," he said, and they all found chairs. Then he took Bedelia by the arm, and together they stepped out to the middle of the floor. "We have somethin' to tell you all," he said. Bedelia looked up at him and smiled, admiration showing clearly in her expression. "Me and Bedelia, we mean to be married. Right away."

Frances was in need of supplies. She told Sam she needed to go to the store. Mack overheard, and he said, "Why spend your money? Give me a list, and me and Willis will go get what you need, and a little more to boot."

"You thinkin' about robbin' the store?" Frances asked.

"Sure," said Mack. "We're already wrote-down outlaws in these parts. We might as well get somethin' out of it, don't you think?"

He and Willis and Sam Baker rode up to Barnsdall's Country Store a few miles outside of Cherokee. They tied their horses at the rail out front and walked into the store. There were a few customers inside, and old Barnsdall himself was behind the counter. Willis had Frances's list, and the boys walked around the store picking up things that were on the list, plus a few extras that struck their fancy. When they saw that Barnsdall was free, they took their selections up and put them on the counter. There were a few items that were not out on the shelves, so they told him what else they wanted, and he fetched the items out. They waited while he wrapped up their selections. When everything was ready, Barnsdall totaled up the cost. Mack pulled out his Starr revolver and pointed it at Barnsdall. "You boys go on ahead and load this stuff up," he said, and Willis and Sam grabbed armloads and left the store. "Now, Mr. Barnsdall," Mack said, "I'll just relieve you of that there cashbox."

"Mack," said Barnsdall, "what is this? Do you know what you're doing?"

"I reckon I do, Mr. Barnsdall. Hell, you know I'm a wanted man already. Me and my brother, we ain't got nothin' to lose, so just hand me that box, and don't make me shoot you."

Barnsdall handed the cashbox to Mack and stepped back, putting his hands up in the air. Mack took the box and backed out of the store. Willis and Sam were mounted already with all of their goods. Mack vaulted into his saddle. They turned their horses and rode away from the store.

The boys cut trees for logs to use in building a cabin back behind Sam and Frances's house. They put up a substantial one-room structure. It was all that Willis and Bedelia would need for a while, for it would be for just the two of them. It was far enough behind the house for privacy yet close enough for a good yell to get attention. When the cabin was finished, the well dug, and the outhouse completed, they started building the furniture. Once again, they did not need much, and it was all completed in a short time.

Then there was no need to wait any longer, so the wedding was planned. It would be at Jenny's house. Willis rode for the preacher. Preacher Harp was a bit unsettled by the appearance of Willis Brooks at his door, but Willis was a perfect gentleman as he let Harp know what he had come for. A deal was struck and a date set, and Willis rode away leaving Harp unharmed.

In just a few days, the wedding took place at Jenny's house. People were invited from miles around. Willis's mind was on only one thing, but Mack and Sam were talking to several young men, and before the day was done, they had three new recruits for the Brooks gang, bringing the total up to six. The wedding went off without a hitch. Preacher Harp did it up in grand style, but he was not too long-winded, either. Jenny was thrilled, and she was already looking forward to grandchildren. Mack was wondering why his baby brother had found a woman before he himself had—and a good-looking one at that. He was jealous. When the wedding was done, the preacher was paid, and he was thrilled at the amount given him by Willis Brooks.

The wedding feast was grand. Everyone attending knew, of course, of the reputation of the Brooks boys, but no one seemed to mind. They just enjoyed the food and drink, and in a perverse way, they enjoyed being the guests of the notorious outlaws. When the last guest was gone, Willis and Bedelia climbed into Sam's buggy and drove to their new home behind the Baker house, where they enjoyed a delightful wedding night.

The honeymoon was short, though. Midmorning of the next day, Mack came to the new house shouting for Willis. Aggravated, Willis pulled on his trousers, crept to the door in his bare feet, and jerked it open, glaring out at his brother. "What the hell is this all about?" he demanded.

"Get dressed and get your guns," Mack said. "Williams and Eastlake's back."

Willis's mood quickly changed, for Williams and Eastlake were the last two names on the list Jenny had given her boys, the last two murderers to be killed. When Willis stepped out of the house, dressed and armed, he found his brother and his brother-in-law waiting outside, mounted and with Willis's horse saddled and waiting. Willis was in the saddle quickly. They all turned their horses to the road.

"Where are the bastards?" Willis asked.

"I heard someone at the store say that Eastlake was goin' fishin' this morning," Mack said. "I think I know where he's goin'."

"Well, lead the way," said Willis.

They rode a few miles down the road, getting close in to Cherokee, when Mack led them off the road onto a narrow trail. They all knew that he was headed for a nearby creek. The trail wound through thick woods. Usually it was only wide enough for one horse, so they rode in single file. Soon Mack stopped riding and dismounted. The others did the same. They walked from that point until they came to the creek. There was no sign of Eastlake.

Mack stepped down close to the water and looked up and down the bank. "I see him," he said, pointing to his left, "way down yonder a ways."

"So how do we get to him?" said Sam. "We go crashin' through the woods, he'll damn sure hear us comin'."

"There's another trail down there," Willis said. "We ride back out on the road and take it."

"Well, let's get it on," said Sam.

They walked back to their horses, mounted, and turned them around. Soon they were back on the road. It wasn't far down to the next trail, and it wasn't long before they were dismounted again and walking toward the creek. They moved slowly and carefully, doing their best to not make a sound. Mack was in the lead. When he spotted Eastlake sitting near the water with his line out and a jug on the ground beside him, he held up a hand and everyone stopped. The creek was lined with rocks, and Mack spotted one behind Eastlake that was about the size of a large cantaloupe. Carefully, he laid down his rifle. He turned and made a sign to the others to keep quiet. Then he crept forward, picked up the rock, raised it high, and brought it crashing down on top of Eastlake's head. It made a sickening sound, and Eastlake made a whuffing noise. He dropped his pole and lay back on the rocks. He may have been senseless, but he was not yet dead.

Mack stood over him, watching him writhe and listening to him moan. Again he raised the rock high, and this time he threw it down with all his might, bashing in the face of the hated man. He bent over to pick up the rock, bloody as it was, and toss it down once again on the already unrecognizable face of his hapless victim.

Willis stepped up, staring wide-eyed. "Is he dead?" he asked.

Mack gave his brother a look. "What the hell do you think?" he said.

Drawing out his long knife, Mack knelt beside the body. "I'll just make sure," he said, and with one long motion, he sliced the throat almost from ear to ear. He wiped the knife blade on Eastlake's trouser leg and put it away. Then he looked at the jug beside the body. He picked it up, uncorked it, took a sniff, then tipped it back to take a long slug. Sam had come up by then, and Willis reached for the jug. Mack handed it over, and Willis took a long drink, then handed it over to Sam, who tipped back his head and took a long pull.

Willis had knelt down beside the ghastly-looking body again. He struck a match and held it to the bottom of one of Eastlake's trouser legs. Soon the trousers started to burn. He moved to the other leg and did the same. "This'll help," said Mack, and he poured some of the contents of the jug onto Eastlake's shirt. Willis struck a second match and lit the shirt. Mack took another drink and passed the jug back to Sam. Gathered around the blazing corpse, they passed the jug around till it was empty. Then they tossed it into the creek and staggered back to their horses. Sherm Williams was forgotten for the time being.

1876

Many months passed. In the spring of 1871, Bedelia had a baby boy, and they named him Henry. It was a difficult birth, and there would be no more children. Two more men had joined the gang, and they were still using Colbert County as their personal fiefdom, raiding and robbing as they pleased. Sherm Williams was still at large, and that fact ate away at the minds of Willis and Mack, and even Sam. It seemed that Williams, fearful for his life, had left the country again. No one seemed to know where he had gone. So finishing up the business they had sworn to take care of for their mother was put on hold.

Henry grew up spoiled and ornery. He was Jenny's first grandchild, and her constant delight. She loved to dandle him on her knee, to bake goodies for him, and to take him for long walks in the woods. One day while Henry was visiting at Jenny's house, he reached for the skull on the table. "Just leave it there, Henry," Jenny said.

"What is it, Mamaw?" Henry asked.

"Well, son," she said, reaching for the lad and pulling him up onto her lap, "it's the head bone of a mean old man."

"Who was he?"

Jenny then told her grandson the tale of what had happened to Willis Sr., his grandpa, and how her sons had gone after the killers. "They got 'em all but one," she said. "Your paw and Uncle Mack did, and one of these days they'll get that last one, too. You wait and see."

"When I get a little bit bigger," Henry said, "I'll get him for you, Mamaw."

She hugged him close and said, "I know you would, my little darlin'. I know you'd do it for me."

Waiting for word about Sherm Williams, the Brooks gang grew restless. One day, Mack proposed robbing the stagecoach as it was on its way into Cherokee. Everyone agreed gleefully. They all readied their weapons and their horses. Willis kissed Bedelia goodbye, and Sam kissed Frances. Henry, five years old now, set up a howl wanting to go along. Leaving Henry squalling, the gang rode off to lay an ambush for the stage. They knew its schedule, knew about when it would be coming down the road. Mack divided the gang into two groups of four each and placed them in hidden spots on both sides of the road. Then they settled down to wait.

They did not have to wait very long. Soon the stage came lumbering up the road, slowing down as it approached the place of ambush because it was going up a hill. Drawing out their pistols, Mack and Willis stepped out into the road. The surprised driver hauled back on the reins. "Whoa. Whoa there," he called, and the horses came to a stop. "What is this?" he asked.

The rest of the gang stepped out, guns in hands. "What the hell does it look like to you?" Mack replied.

"I'd say it looks like a holdup."

"You're damn right," said Mack. "Toss down your cashbox and your mailbag."

The driver tossed them down. In the meantime, Willis ordered the passengers out of the coach. There was an older woman and a young woman, and there were three men, all dressed in suits. Willis produced a bag and ordered everyone to put their valuables in it. When they all had complied, Willis patted the men down to make sure they had not tried to cheat him. He found a small handgun hidden under one coat, and he held it up in front of its owner's face. "Was you thinkin' of doing somethin' with this here little peashooter?" he asked.

"Why, no, I wasn't."

"Whyn't you drop it in the sack?"

"I didn't think it was worth anything to you."

Willis dropped it in the bag. "I'll be the judge of that," he said.

Mack unhitched the horses and slapped the two leads on the haunch. They ran ahead on the road. "I reckon that'll slow you up some," he said.

"Hey," said the driver, "how am I supposed to get this thing on into town?"

"You'll just have to try to catch them nags," Mack said. Then in a louder voice, he called out, "Let's get outta here, boys."

The gang rode away with their loot, leaving the driver and the passengers to chase the horses and find their way into town as best they could.

It was a couple of hours later when the stage finally rolled into town. It was met by a small crowd of curious folks wondering why it was so late.

"Where you been, Charlie?" someone asked the driver.

"You're late," said another.

"Got held up," Charlie said. "It was them Brookses."

"The Brooks gang?"

"That's what I said. It was them, all right."

"They ain't never done that before."

"Stagecoach ain't never been robbed."

"Somebody fetch Alex Heflin over here."

The sheriff arrived shortly and began questioning the driver and the passengers. He was soon assured that the robbery had indeed been perpetrated by the Brooks gang.

"You've got to put a stop to this, Alex," someone said. "The sooner the better."

"Them Brookses is runnin' this county."

"Robbin' and killin' as they please."

"We can't have this. No one is safe around here no more."

"We need a new sheriff is what we need."

Then someone stepped up to one of the passengers who had just disembarked and said, "Say, Sherm, is that you?"

"Yeah. How're you doin'?"

"I'm just fine. It's good to see you back here. You here to stay this time?"

"Not sure yet, Merv. I see the Brooks boys is still active."

Jenny Brooks had driven her wagon over to the Baker place. Of course, they had seen her coming, and her two sons and Sam all met the wagon. Mack helped her down. "Hello, Maw," he said. "This is a nice surprise."

"You might not think so when I tell you why I come," Jenny said.

"What's wrong, Mama?" asked Willis.

"Hi, Mama." It was Frances, who had just come out of the house wiping her hands on a dishcloth. She hurried up and gave her mother a hug.

Jenny extricated herself as quickly as she could. Then she looked sternly around at the boys. "Boys," she said, "do you recollect swearin' a solemn oath to me the day they kilt your daddy?"

"Sure, Maw," said Mack, "we remember it well."

"We ain't never forgot it, Mama," said Willis. "We done kilt six of those seven bastards. What's wrong?"

"When you boys robbed that stagecoach the other day," Jenny said, "one of the passengers on it was Sherm Williams. You rode off and never touched him. Not a one of you. You never touched a hair on his head."

The boys, taken aback, shuffled nervously. Then Willis said, "It was me that robbed the passengers, Mama. I never recognized him, or else I'da kilt him. I never did know him too good."

She turned on Mack. "I s'pose you never recognized him, neither," she said.

"I woulda," he said, "but I never really got a look at the passengers. I guess I was too busy up front. But we'll find him and kill him fer certain."

"I sure do hope so," said Jenny, "cause your father and your big brother ain't goin' to rest till you do. He's the last one, you know. When you get him, it'll all be over and done with."

"We'll get him, Mama," said Mack, "but it won't be over and done with. It won't ever be over and done with till we're all dead and buried."

Mack sent out all the gang except for Willis and Sam to search for Sherm Williams. A few days later, one of the newer members of the gang came to Mack and told him that he had received word that Williams had gone to Allen's Factory in Franklin County. It was a thread mill, and Williams had some sort of business deal he wanted to propose over there. Mack called Willis and Sam together. They said they did not need the rest of the gang.

After a hard ride, they found Allen's Factory, and they saw that a buggy was parked in front. "That must be Williams's," said Mack. They dismounted and tied their horses to the rail in front. Then they lounged around in the yard waiting. Mack indulged in his newest habit. He rolled himself a cigarette and sat there looking grim as he smoked it. Willis had his six-gun out and was playing with it. Sam trimmed his nails with a pocketknife.

"How damn long we goin' to sit here?" asked Mack. "We been hangin' around here for forty-five minutes now."

"He's got to come out sometime," said Willis.

"I'm damn tired of waitin'," Mack said.

"We've waited all this time," said Willis. "We can wait a little longer."

The front door of the factory was opened from the inside, and two men stepped out. Willis recognized one of them as the man he had taken the pocket pistol away from during the stagecoach robbery. The other man stuck out his hand to shake and said, "Thank you, Mr. Williams. We'll be in touch with you real soon now."

"Thank you, sir," Williams said. "Goodbye now."

The other man went back inside, and Williams headed for the rig, barely taking notice of the three men lounging around. Mack tossed aside what was left of his cigarette and stepped toward the rig. "Mr. Williams," he said.

Williams looked at Mack. "Yes? What is it?"

"I did hear that feller call you Williams, didn't I?"

"That's right."

"Are you Sherm Williams?"

"That's me. Who wants to know?"

Mack pulled out his Starr revolver. "Mack Brooks," he said. "Son of Willis Sr., brother to John." He fired. The bullet tore into Williams's left hip. Williams yelped in pain and surprise.

Willis stepped up, firing his Remington. "And I'm Willis Jr."

Williams was down on his knees by this time, hit by three bullets. He was bleeding from the hip, from a shoulder, and from the chest. He was coughing and spitting blood. Sam came forward. "Sam Baker, Mr. Williams. I'm an in-law." He fired, his shot catching Williams in the forehead. Williams pitched forward and lay dead.

The factory door opened again, and the same man who had come out with Williams earlier stepped out to see what was going on. Mack fired a shot in his direction, hitting the wall behind him. The man shrieked and ran back inside. "Let's go see Mama, boys," Mack said.

Jenny sat and rocked when her sons gave her the news. Inside she was thrilled, but outside she didn't show it. "So they're all gone," she said. "At last. Willis and John can rest now. You boys did fine." She rocked. "Are you hungry? Can I fetch you up a meal?"

"We ain't hungry, Mama," said Mack.

"I might could drink some coffee," said Willis.

"Coffee sounds good," Mack agreed.

"Yeah," said Sam.

Jenny heaved herself up out of the rocker and went to prepare the coffee. She was nearing fifty years old, and she had waited thirteen years for this moment. She almost wished that she had told the boys to bring her all of the heads. She could have had seven skulls lined up on her table. Oh well. She would just be satisfied that the seven damned Tories were dead. The seven murdering bastards who had killed her Willis and John. They were dead, and all at the hands of her boys. She had the best boys in the whole damn world.

Willis became restless. The job was done. The seven men were dead. He did not think that he was cut out for the outlaw's life. He tried to think of where he could go or what he could do. He wanted to get away with Bedelia and Henry and lead a normal and honest life, but he knew he would have to go far from Alabama before he could even think about not being recognized. He would have to change his name. He grew angrier every day when he saw Mack and Sam enjoying more and more their lives as outlaws, relishing in the knowledge that they were feared for miles around. Especially since Sam, too, was a father now. He and Frances had a boy, Tom, born four years earlier, about a year after Henry was born. The Brooks gang. It made him sick to his stomach.

1878

Jenny was proud of her boys. She had raised a couple of outlaws, but it was the fault of the damned Tories. They had started it all. As far as Jenny was concerned, the war had never ended. Not the Civil War nor the war between the Cherokees and the United States. Her boys were still fighting it, and they would continue. It would never be over to Jenny.

The people of the town of Cherokee were getting fed up, however, as were the residents of the entire county. Many of them met at the office of Sheriff Heflin one morning to demand that action be taken against the Brooks gang. Heflin said that he needed some proof before he could arrest the Brooks boys or any of the members of their so-called gang. The crowd insisted that everyone knew who they were and what they had done. The argument raged on for some time until Heflin finally gave in.

"All right," he finally said. "So we know. But I can't just ride out to their hangout and arrest them. There's too many of them. They'd just shoot me down, and that would be the end of it."

"We can form up a damned big posse," said one of the crowd.

"We can plan the whole thing like a military operation," said another.

A few days later, Sheriff Heflin led a posse of a dozen men out toward the Baker-Brooks place. They were close by sundown, and he stopped them and made a camp for the night. His plan was to strike with the first morning light. They built some small fires and made some coffee. One of the men pulled out a bottle of whiskey, and Heflin took it away from him and smashed the bottle. "There'll be none of that," he said. He gave the man a cup of coffee. He had everyone check their weapons, and they turned in early.

When the sun had barely peeped over the horizon, he roused everyone. They saddled their horses and made one last check of their weapons. They had some coffee and some cold biscuits. Then they mounted up. They rode about a mile before Heflin sent two men on ahead. As planned, the two men climbed the hill on their left and made their way to a spot above the Brookses' lookout post. Then they worked their way down until they could see the guard. They had thought that one of them would sneak down behind him with a knife and kill him quietly, but looking down, they could see that there was no way. The hillside was too steep, and it was covered with loose rocks. They would have to shoot, and it had been agreed that a shot would signal the rest of the posse to attack.

The guard was sitting cross-legged behind a boulder, holding a Winchester rifle, watching the road below. Up above him, one of the two posse men pulled out a Colt revolver and cocked it. He took careful aim and fired, the bullet smashing into the guard's back. The guard turned halfway around and fired the Winchester, but the shot went wild, and he pitched forward dead.

Down below, but still back far enough so as not to be seen from the lookout post, the posse heard the shots. Heflin pulled out a rifle and shouted, "Let's go!" The ten men spurred their horses and rode hard toward the houses and barn of the Brooks gang. Mack had heard the shots and was the first one out of bed. He pulled on his trousers and grabbed a six-gun—the Starr revolver he had carried all these years—then ran out of the house looking for whoever had fired the shots.

Just then, the posse came pounding up into the yard. Mack fired, hitting one of the riders and knocking him out of the saddle. The other posse men all commenced firing at him, hitting him several times. But he was hard to kill. He jerked each time a bullet hit him. He kept firing back, but his shots were all wild. Sam had also gotten up by then and started firing from the doorway of the house. He hit two of the attackers. Mack stumbled over the fallen men and did not move again.

The rest of the posse all dismounted and ran for cover. Some hid behind trees; some got down behind a wagon that was sitting in the yard. Other members of the gang were firing now, mostly from the barn, but they couldn't really see what they were shooting at. The exchange of shots slowed down. Willis had made his way to the Baker house, and he and Sam were firing from there. Frances was reloading their guns.

Bedelia had seen Mack fall, and from inside her house, she was screaming obscenities at the posse and encouragement to the members of the gang. "Kill all of the dirty bastards," she shrieked. "Mack and Willis would kill them all. They'd kill you, too, if you don't fight hard enough. You're cowards if you don't kill them. Kill the bastards!"

The posse fired shots into Willis and Bedelia's house, using Bedelia's voice as their target. When more shots came from the barn, they fired back at the barn. Henry, all of seven years old, kept shouting, "Get 'em, Mama, kill 'em all!"

From his place behind the wagon in the yard, Heflin shouted out an order: "Don't waste your shots, men! Make sure you hit what you're aimin' at."

"Mama," Henry said, "I can't see good from here. I'm goin' over to Sam's house." He opened the door and started to run.

"No! Get back!" screamed Bedelia, reaching for him as he opened the door. But she was too late. She screamed after him just the same.

"Henry, come back in here! Henry, it ain't safe out there!" He had taken only a few steps when a shot from behind the wagon hit him in the leg, shattering his knee. He screamed and went down hard. She saw him stumble and started toward him, then felt a burning in her chest as a bullet struck her. Henry rolled around in the grass for a time before passing out from loss of blood.

Two of the men who had been recruited into the gang suddenly came out of the barn on horseback, racing as fast as they could go toward the road to town. A man in the posse fired a shot, knocking one of them out of the saddle. The other made good his escape.

By midmorning, Heflin, realizing that he had lost three men and that the posse had killed only Mack and maybe young Henry, decided to call it quits. "We've done enough, men," he said. "Let's get to our horses and get the hell out of here." Almost as one man, they broke for their horses and mounted, heading back to Cherokee as fast as they could go. Unbeknownst to Heflin and the posse, the Brooks gang was broken. As soon as the coast was clear, Sam rode hard for a doctor.

When Willis realized that Bedelia was dead, he felt something drain out of him. Holding her, he felt nothing but loss. The doctor came and amputated Henry's right leg. There was nothing more he could do, he said. There was too much damage.

The gang members who were not part of the family had all left. There was no one at home anymore but Willis, one-legged Henry, Sam and Frances, and young Tom. They had a family meeting and decided that it was time to get out of Colbert County. They drove their wagon to Cherokee and bought train tickets to Texas. If Alex Heflin was in town, he was apparently unaware that the remnants of the Brooks gang were boarding a train west. If he knew, he thought it best to stay quietly in his office. Sam and Willis carried Henry on a cot.

When the train reached Preston, Texas, they all disembarked. With what was left of their ill-gotten gains, they purchased a small farm outside of town, and they settled down to try their hands at farming. They did not do well. Willis had fashioned a peg leg for Henry with padding on the top and straps to hold it in place. Henry happily threw away the crutch he had been using and struggled for a few days learning to hobble on the new wooden leg. He did his best to help with the farm work, but he couldn't do much. The only consolation he had was that Willis and Sam weren't doing much better. They refused to admit, though, that they just weren't cut out for farm work. After a few years, they came to the conclusion that the land in North Texas was no good for farming, and they decided to move north into Indian Territory.

Willis settled near Grady in the Chickasaw Nation. It was 1882. The soil was fertile and the grass was good, but even so, Willis decided that pushing a plow wasn't the life for him. He went back into Texas and stole some horses, which he used to start a herd in the Chickasaw Nation. Then in 1885 he moved with Henry and his small horse herd to Dogtown, near Eufaula, in the Creek Nation. He settled in a location with good grass, and his herd began to grow. He was actually prosperous now and thought he might have found his calling.

1889

Sam Baker had had a long talk with Willis some years earlier. He and Frances had decided that they would be less likely to be recognized by anyone if they were not all together, so they had moved to Collinsville in the Cherokee Nation. Their son, Tom, was now seventeen years old, and he was already running with a bad crowd. One of Tom's friends was a killer named Jim McFarland. Tom and McFarland headed up a rough bunch that terrorized the area around Claremore. There was some confusion among the locals as to whether it was the Baker gang or the McFarland gang. This confusion led to bad feelings between Tom and McFarland.

One day McFarland approached Tom. "Say, Tom," he said, "you know that Old Man Weaver?"

"The old retired Texas Ranger who lives on Texanna Road?"

"Yeah, that one. You know, he lives all by hisself, and they say he has a bunch of money hid around his house. He don't trust banks."

"Is that right?"

"Yeah. It oughta be easy to get that money offa him some night."

Tom scratched his head. "Yeah," he said. "It oughta."

Tom Baker rode up to the home of Old Man Weaver after dark. He tied his horse to the fence in front of the house and dismounted. Pulling his six-gun out of its holster, he opened the gate and walked toward the front door. Unbeknownst to Tom, Weaver was looking out his front window and saw a man approaching his house with a drawn gun. As Tom stepped up onto the porch, the front door swung open, and Weaver appeared in the doorway, Colt in hand and leveled at Tom. Weaver shot four times, each shot hitting in a close pattern in Tom's chest. Tom fell back off the porch dead.

Shooter and victim were both thought to be white, and so the Creek Nation's law enforcement agencies were not allowed jurisdiction. Deputy marshals from Fort Smith, Arkansas, investigated. The association between Tom Baker and Jim McFarland was well known, so the marshals questioned McFarland. McFarland said, "I don't know nothin' about it. I guess ole Tom got the idee he could pull off that job by hisself, and he just got kilt tryin' it." When the marshals went to question Sam Baker, he said, "Everyone around here knows that my boy was runnin' with that damned no-good Jim McFarland. McFarland must of dreamed up the scheme and somehow talked Tom into tryin' to pull it off by hisself. Then he went and warned Old Man Weaver, so that Weaver would be waitin' for Tom when he come around. That's what happened." So it was Jim McFarland's word against Sam Baker's word. No action was taken.

Henry Brooks, now nineteen, had in spite of his handicap struck out on his own. He went to Clayton, in the Choctaw Nation, where he found employment in the logging camps. He could handle a team of horses pretty well. His peg leg did not bother him on a wagon seat, and he was doing all right. Everyone around called him Peg Leg Brooks. That was all right with Henry. It made him sound like a pirate, and he liked that.

He was hitching up his team one day when another wagon pulled up beside him. "Howdy, Dickey," said Henry. Dickey set his brake handle and climbed down out of his wagon.

"Brooks," he said, "I sure do admire them horses of yours. You want to swap me for mine?"

"Can't say I do, Dickey. I'm happy with these two."

"I bet you are, but I sure do want them for myself. I'll give you my two horses and ten dollars to boot."

"You'd have to make it more than that," Henry said. They agreed on fifteen dollars, and the trade was made.

It was a few days later when Henry was stopped by two deputy U.S. marshals. He was driving his new team. "These your horses, Peg Leg?" asked one of the deputies.

"Yep, they're mine," Henry said.

"Then you're under arrest," said the other deputy.

"What for?"

"They're stolen."

"Wait a minute. I traded my horses to ole Dickey. Find him and ask him."

"Dickey's left the country. We believe he was part of a gang of horse thieves workin' around here, and it looks to us like you was a part of it, too."

On May 12, 1890, Henry "Peg Leg" Brooks was convicted of horse stealing and sentenced to ten years at Leavenworth, 1890 to 1899. When Jenny got word of the sentencing, she got in touch with Willis, and together they hired a lawyer from Muskogee named Cravens.

1904

Henry had been in prison for four years when Lawyer Cravens finally won his appeal. He had argued that there was no proof that Henry was part of a gang of horse thieves that included the elusive Dickey, and the most that he should have been charged with was receiving stolen property. Henry was released, and he went straight back to Dogtown and the still-growing herd of horses. He wrote to his grandmother in Cherokee, Alabama, to tell her the news.

Jenny, who by this time was known to one and all in Colbert County as Aunt Jenny, was thrilled with the letter. Since Mack's death, her grandson Henry had been Jenny's "Cherokee boy." Henry told her that he had been pardoned and thanked her for her help in acquiring the services of Cravens. He said that he had survived his four years in the pen very well. He was healthy and feeling well, but he was especially happy to be a free man once again. He told her that he was back home with his father in Dogtown. Everything was just fine.

Aunt Jenny felt happy for her favorite. She would have loved to see him, but travel was out of the question for her. She had lived in the same house now since before the Civil War. She figured she was about seventy-five years old by this time, and she had been living alone for some twenty-five years. She did everything for herself. She chopped her own wood. She butchered her own hogs. She gathered her own wild greens and grew her own garden. She sold some things from her garden for enough money to buy coffee and tobacco for her corncob pipe. That was about all she needed from the store.

Aunt Jenny had become a respected person around Colbert County. Since they had gotten rid of her sons, the people liked Jenny once again. She was one of the oldest settlers of the county. She lived alone and took care of herself. And then there was that skull that sat on her kitchen table. Few, if any, had actually seen it, but everyone had heard about it. It was said to belong to the man who had killed her husband, and her sons had killed that man and cut off his head, and they all believed it. It might be said that Aunt Jenny was the pride of Colbert County.

For years there had been rumors about how Willis had started his herd by stealing horses. But early on, those stories likely did him more good than harm. After all, the horses had been stolen from Texas, and that wasn't all bad. But the rumors followed him to Dogtown, and as his herd grew, so did the stories. There were those who resented his success, and when they got wind that his son had been convicted of stealing horses in Clayton, that gave new life to the rumors in the minds of many, and fed their resentment. Among them was Max Thorson. Max had been dealing in horses for years, but had never been able to make much of a go of it. He took Willis's success as a personal insult, and it rankled him more and more as the years passed.

The final straw for Max came when Henry was cleared of the charge and released from prison. He finally decided to do something about it, to "cut Willis down to size," as he put it. Max knew a couple of men who shared his feelings toward Willis, and he went to them with a proposal.

"What say we give Willis a taste of his own medicine? He don't deserve that big herd of his, so let's just help ourselfs to some of it."

"You proposin' we turn horse thieves?" asked Luke Strayer.

"Why not?" Max said. "Seems fair enough to me."

"What's fair 'bout thievin' from Willis? What's he ever did to us?" asked Strayer.

"He'd hardly miss 'em," chimed in Bud Vickery.

"That ain't the point, damn it! Don't you want some of what is just as rightly yourn as his'n?" asked Max, his patience wearing thin.

"It still don't seem worth the risk," said Vickery.

"What risk? Ain't nobody gonna get hurt," snapped Max.

"I don't know," said Strayer. "How do ya propose we set about it?"

Thorson's plan was simple enough. They'd go at night, take down a few rails from the corral fence, and wait till some horses drifted out. All they had to do was keep quiet and not spook the herd. They'd round up maybe twenty or so horses and take off.

It didn't quite turn out that way. Willis and his son were sitting up late talking, still catching up on all that had happened since Henry had left home. They had talked comfortably till long into the evening, not even bothering to light a lamp. So when Thorson and his two companions approached Willis's place, it looked as if no one was up and about.

Dismounting and leaving their horses with Strayer, Max and Vickery crossed quietly to the corral and set to work. But as they lifted off the top rail, Vickery felt a cough coming on. Trying to stifle it, he jerked his head, and the rail slipped out of his grasp, striking his knee. "Damn!" he yelled through clenched teeth. Well, not exactly yelled, but despite his effort, he couldn't muffle it completely. It was just loud enough to catch Willis's attention, and he got up to investigate. When he crossed the room and opened the door, Max panicked and let go one shot, calling to his accomplices to hightail it out of there.

The shot caught Willis square in the chest, and by the time Henry reached him, he was breathing his last. Henry couldn't, of course, make out who it was riding away. Not that it would have made any difference, since he wouldn't have known them anyway. So Max Thorson and his boys didn't get their horses after all. But Max had been right about one thing: there wasn't any risk to them. They were never caught and held accountable.

Henry "Peg Leg" Brooks had no reason to remain in the Indian Nations. So before too long he sold the herd, packed his belongings in a wagon, and headed east, back to Alabama. Jenny was happy to see him, and when he first arrived at her house, she fed him a mighty meal. News of Willis's death had already reached her, and she'd had some time to get over it. The sight of Henry helped her overcome what lingered of her grief. He was her Cherokee boy, and Jenny loved him dearly.

Henry soon learned that all of the old charges and bad feelings against the Brooks boys in Colbert County were now a thing of the past, but something of their old reputation still lingered. Still, in spite of his missing leg, he managed to get an appointment as deputy sheriff of Colbert County.

Henry was now thirty-four years old and ready to settle down. He married a local girl, and they moved into their own house, bought with what was left of the money he'd gotten for the herd. But he soon discovered that his pay as deputy sheriff was not enough for them to live on, so he built a still and started making whiskey and selling it. At first it was only to locals in Colbert County, but as word spread, customers started coming from Lawrence County as well. In a couple of years, he was even making occasional runs for the convenience of customers from neighboring Winston County. He had always been quick to anger, and more than once he had been known to club a man who was slow to pay for his whiskey. He was especially hard on those from Winston County, which was known to have been a Tory hangout during the Civil War. Henry remembered the stories he'd heard growing up about what the Tories had done to his papaw and his Uncle John, stories that even now Mamaw Jenny kept retelling.

On January 20, 1910, Henry Brooks was driving his wagon down a lonely road in Lawrence County when twelve men suddenly blocked his path. Henry's rifle was across his knee. He put a hand on it and eyed the men with suspicion. All old Tories, he thought. All from Winston County. He even recognized a couple whose heads he had bashed at one time or another. He also noticed that each of the twelve men had a gun in his hand.

"What do you men want?" he asked.

"You're a crooked lawman," said one.

"We know you're sellin' whiskey," said another. "Makin' it, too."

"So what do you intend doin' about it?" Henry said.

"We mean to kill you, you peg-legged bastard."

Henry started to raise his Winchester, but he was stopped by a bullet in his chest. Each man fired in turn, riddling Henry's body with twelve bullets.

When Aunt Jenny was informed about Henry's death, she only said, "They all died with their boots on, like men." She sat rocking on her porch and thinking over the last fifty or so years of her life, thinking about the number of killings of her own family and the number of killings they had done. A lot of men, she thought. A lot were dead. And what had started it all, what had caused it all, was the deliberate murder of her husband, Willis, and her firstborn son, John, by those damned Tories. Had it all been worth it? Of course it had been. She couldn't have let a thing like that go unpunished.

She got up and went back in her house to look at the skull, which still sat on her table, but right beside it now lay her grandson Henry's wooden peg leg. "When I finally go," she thought, "I'll have them two things buried with me." Then she sat down with a cup of coffee and took a sip. Setting the cup down on the table, she stared at the skull. "If I'da been a man," she told herself, "there'd be a whole lot more dead."

Rachel's Child

I had been reading the latest copy of the *Advocate* and was mildly irritated, having found several typographical errors, when I heard the sound of hoofbeats approaching my house. I glanced over the paper in my hands and saw my wife, Rachel, at the window.

"Who is it?" I asked.

"Ju wa," she said.

"What?"

"It's Water Dog."

I tossed aside the *Advocate* and came up quickly from my chair.

"You stay there," she said. "I can take care of this."

I didn't like the feeling that my wife, in a time of danger, would tell me to stay in the background. It seemed to me that I should go outside and confront this threat to our happy home life, but she spoke with such authority that I sensed that I had better obey her.

"Where's the boy?" I asked. For some reason, I could never bring myself to call her son by his name.

"He's out back. He's okay."

I went to my desk and opened a side drawer to remove my .44 revolver.

"Stay back out of sight," said Rachel.

I decided that I'd do as she said as long as it was apparent that she really could handle the situation without my interference. Water Dog was the father of her child, the boy I had just asked about, and though they were not married, had never been, Water Dog had mercilessly harassed and tormented the poor woman for a period of ten years before I had even met her. As he approached the house that day, he was unaware of my presence. His home was some thirty miles away in another district, and I had just recently married Rachel and moved in with her and the child. If Water Dog tried to force his way into the house to bother her, he would find me there ready for him. My heart was pounding with anticipation as I positioned myself against the front wall, my gun in hand. He wouldn't see me unless he came into the house, I thought. I almost hoped that he would come in and give me an excuse to kill him. I hated the man, though I had never in my life set eyes on him. I hated him for the things he had done to Rachel. She had told me about some of his cruelty, and I had no use for a man who would mistreat a woman. And this man's treatment of the woman who had just become my wife had been especially cruel. I wanted to kill him, yet my body betrayed my own fear to me. I had never killed a man.

Rachel opened the door. "What do you want?" she asked.

He answered her in the Cherokee language, which I did not understand, but he must have asked about the boy.

"He's not home right now," said Rachel.

He said something else in a surly and demanding voice. I was taking slow, deep breaths and noticed that my fingers and palm on the pistol grip were sweating.

"I don't have to tell you anything. Get away from here," Rachel said.

"You don't think so, huh?" said Water Dog, suddenly changing to English, and I heard the creak of saddle leather and imagined that he was climbing down off his horse. Then came the sound of footsteps. I raised the revolver and aimed it toward the door. As I did that, I saw him, or rather, his reflection, just for an instant, looming up in the mirror that hung on the wall on the opposite side of the door from where I waited. Just as his image appeared, Rachel stepped quickly back and slammed the door. There was a loud banging on the outside of the door as if he had bashed it with his fist. He laughed out loud. Then he mounted his horse and rode away at a gallop. It occurred to me that if I had seen him, he might also have seen me with my gun in that same mirror, and that was what had kept him out of the house. I walked to the door and put my arms around Rachel.

"He's gone," she said.

"He's lucky," I said. "I'd have killed him if he'd come through that door."

It was only then that I looked up and saw little Round Hair standing at the back wall in a direct line from the front door. He stood with his arms crossed, his bare feet slightly apart, and I wondered, how long had he been there? I didn't know. He had been, as his mother had said, "out back." I had not heard him come back in. Almost as quickly as I saw him, he turned and ran for the back door and was out again. I shuddered at the look in his eyes, and then I wondered if Water Dog had also seen the boy. I wondered, after all, if it had been my reflection in the mirror or the hard, cold stare of his own small son that had driven the wretch back just as he had been ready to burst into my home. The thought was absurd, and I shook it out of my head and went back to my newspaper.

I had returned to the Cherokee Nation in the spring of 1892. I say "returned" though I had never seen it before. My grandfather had taken his wife and son (my father at ten years of age) to California with other Cherokees to search for gold in 1850. Like most of the searchers, he had worn himself out with the quest and died penniless and disappointed. My father, a mixed-blood, grew to manhood in that country, ironically known to Cherokees as *adel juhdlv* (they get money out of there). He married at twenty, and within a year, I was born. I grew up in that western land, was educated in the schools there, and became a journalist. From my grandfather, I had heard a few tales of the Cherokee Nation, and I had always wanted to see it. I knew, of course, that I was Cherokee, though I looked white, and at the age of thirty-two, having read about the troubles the Cherokees were having with the United States government and the movement for abolition of the tribal government, the proposed allotment of Cherokee lands to individual tribal members, and the establishment of Indian Territory in preparation for the creation of a new state, I quit my job and headed east.

It hadn't been difficult for me to obtain employment with the *Cherokee Advocate.* W. P. Boudinot, the editor, was overjoyed to find a tribal member with substantial journalistic experience. He put me right to work as a copyeditor and reporter. It was there that I met the woman who would soon become my wife. Rachel was the secretary and general office manager for the *Advocate,* and a more efficient one I had never known. She was a beautiful full-blood Cherokee woman with smooth brown skin and long, straight, shining black hair. I believe that I fell in love with her at once.

At first I talked with her about politics, and I found her to be remarkably well informed, not only about local tribal politics, but also about the politicians in Washington. There was a strong movement afoot to create a new state, and part of that process was to be the dissolution of the tribal governments. Since the Indian tribes, or Nations, did not practice private ownership of land, a necessary first step in this process was to be the drawing up of a "final roll" of the Cherokees and the other affected tribes. This final roll would be used to assign each tribal member an allotment of land. When the new state came into being, there would be no more Cherokee Nation, nor even a Cherokee tribe. There would be, theoretically, no more Cherokee people. There would be only private citizens who were landowners in the new state.

The more traditional Cherokees, mostly full-bloods, were strongly opposed to this plan; however, a large number of mostly mixed-blood Cherokees, known as Progressives, were in favor of it. Though I am a mixed-blood and can in no way call myself traditional, I found myself in opposition to the advocates of statehood.

"We can't let them get away with this," I said to Rachel. "It will destroy the Cherokee Nation."

"They can never destroy the Cherokee people," she answered me, "and that's what really matters."

It wasn't long after my first quick glimpse of Water Dog in the mirror that I went outside my home for a stroll in the sun. Our house was in Park Hill, a lovely little community near Tahlequah, our Nation's capital, and we had near neighbors, yet we maintained a wooded setting with ample space around us. A road ran in front of the house, but behind us was thick woods. Our neighbors were strung out along the road, with similar settings for their homes. I had stepped out the front door and walked to the road and was savoring the sweet spring smells, and I felt myself drawn to the shadows of the trees behind my house. I walked around to the back of the house, and I could see wisps of smoke rising from a thicket nearby. There wasn't enough smoke to alarm me, just enough to arouse my curiosity, so I made my way, somewhat cautiously, to the thicket. Pushing aside some tangles of blackberry, I saw Round Hair. He was smoking a beautifully rolled cigarette. I noticed that most particularly, because every time I have rolled a cigarette, the result has been embarrassingly sloppy. Round Hair sat in a small clearing in the midst of the thorny blackberry, with just enough space for his small body. He sat still, and he smoked deliberately.

"Hey, *chooj*," I said, a bit self-conscious about my use of the Cherokee word for "boy." He answered me only with a look from those very large and nearly black eyes. The expression on his face was blank. It told me nothing. Only the eyes moved and looked at me, I thought, accusingly.

"What are you up to?" I said, and again I felt foolish. I knew what he was doing, of course. He was hiding behind the house and smoking. I had done the same thing when I was not much older than he. All boys do it, I suppose. He stared at me, his eyes, it seemed to me, burning.

"Don't you think you're a bit young to be smoking?" I said dutifully. I was feeling strongly my new role of stepfather. Still he stared, and yet I received no other answer. "Why don't you come on in the house?" I said, and I turned and went to the back door and on inside. The boy did not follow me.

Stalking somewhat indignantly through the house, I called out to Rachel. "Your son is out there smoking," I said.

"Don't worry about it," she answered. "He'll be all right. You take everything too seriously. Why don't you sit down and relax. I'll get you a cup of fresh coffee."

A few days later, I was in the *Advocate* office working on a story about the Cherokee delegation to Washington and their efforts on behalf of the Cherokee Nation. I was in a back room with Rachel, who was at another desk working on some correspondence. Mr. Boudinot was in the outer office. I heard the door open and glanced up and through the doorway between the two rooms to see a full-blood Indian enter whom I did not know.

"Hello," said Mr. Boudinot. "Can I do something for you?"

"I'm Hogshooter," said the stranger.

"I'm W. P. Boudinot, editor of the *Advocate*."

Mr. Boudinot extended his hand, but Hogshooter ignored it.

"I brought a message," he said, "from Water Dog for that new man."

I started to rise from my seat, but Rachel moved quickly to my side and put a hand on my shoulder. "Sit still," she said in a whisper.

"Water Dog says he's coming to this place," said Hogshooter. "He's coming in here, and he's going to kill that man. He says that he's going to do it with his bare hands."

"You tell Water Dog," said Mr. Boudinot, "that he'll have to get past me to do that. Now, get out of here."

Hogshooter left the office, and soon we all went home for lunch. Rachel wasn't needed for the rest of the day, so I walked back to work alone after I had eaten. I was walking down the road that led from my house back to the office, still agitated about the threat I had received from Water Dog. As I approached a blind curve, blind because of the thickness of the woods that grew alongside the road, I could hear hoofbeats coming from the other direction. Suddenly the rider and horse appeared around the bend, and I found myself facing Water Dog. He was as surprised as I at first, but he soon recovered, and with a roar, he kicked his horse into a gallop and made straight at me.

"Hey," I yelled, and to save myself I dove headlong into the ditch beside the road. Water Dog pulled hard on the reins, forcing the horse to stop and then rear, its front hooves flailing the air. The animal's neighs were almost shrieks, and Water Dog laughed. Then he once again kicked the horse forward and raced off down the road, his laughter echoing in my ears. After he had disappeared from sight, I got up and dusted myself off. Then, before returning to work, I walked back home and got out my .44. I carried it with me after that.

It was in the fall of the year. Mr. Boudinot and I were working late in the office. Ned Christie had just been killed by a posse of United States marshals at his home east of Tahlequah. Many Indians were convinced that Christie was killed because of his political beliefs. Of course, the federal government had charges against him, but his supporters claimed that the charges were false. I tended to side with the traditionals on this issue, and I suggested to Mr. Boudinot that our story should include at least some of the speculation that Christie was not an outlaw. He vetoed my suggestion, and, as he not only was writing the story but was also my boss, there was nothing more I could do.

He set me to work going through the files to find some filler. "There's a file in that bottom drawer of interviews with old-timers," he said. "Some of it's just cultural stuff. You know, how the Cherokees used to do this or that? You might find something interesting in there."

I pulled out the drawer and found the file. There was an interview with an old woman who had come over the Trail of Tears and told her story. There was a version of the story of how the Cherokees came into the world as told by an old man who lived out by Fort Gibson. All of it was interesting, but the thing that really got my attention was an old document with the heading "How to Make a Witch." I sat down to read it with care. It said that a mother could make a witch of her own child by following the directions. Without going into detail, it called for the mother to take her newborn infant into isolation for a period of some months and to feed it only the diet specified in the document.

"Mr. Boudinot," I said.

"Yes."

"Have you read all of this file?"

"Yes, I think so."

"This one here, 'How to Make a Witch,' do you know this one?"

"Oh, yes, I remember that one. I don't think we should use that one, though."

"But," I said, a little hesitant, "is it real?"

"Some of our full-bloods are still very superstitious," he said. "It's real. I mean by that, there are people who believe it."

"What kind of a woman would turn her own child into a witch deliberately?"

"Oh, I don't know. One who was greedy, perhaps, and wanted the power through her child to seek personal gain. One who was afraid of something and wanted her child's protection."

I shuddered as I recalled the day Water Dog had nearly broken into my house.

"Mr. Boudinot," I said, "how long have you known my wife?"

"About ten or twelve years, I guess."

"Did you know her before her child was born?"

Boudinot stood up from his work. "Wait a minute," he said. "What are you getting at?"

"Did you?"

"Yes, I did."

"And where was she when the boy was born and for the next several months?"

"I don't know. She left town for a while. I imagine she didn't want to face the reproachful looks of the folks here in town. The boy was born out of wedlock, you know."

"Yes," I said, "it could have been that."

"Now I've got to get back to this story. We still need some filler for the next edition. Put that out of your mind and find something in there that we can use. Okay?"

"Okay," I said, and I did continue to look for filler, although I didn't put my previous thoughts out of my mind. I pulled the story about the first Cherokees, and Boudinot finished what he was working on.

"That's enough for this evening," he said. "We can wrap this up in the morning."

We pulled on our coats and stepped out the front door. I stood there waiting while Boudinot locked the door.

"Are you familiar with Indian names and where they come from?" I said.

"Yeah, some."

"Rachel's boy, Round Hair. What kind of a name is that?"

"It's a rather unusual one," said Boudinot.

"But what does it mean? How is hair round?"

"Oh," he said. "It refers, I think, to a ringlet, a lock of hair that curled."

"What kind of a name is that for a child?" I asked.

"Like I said before, an unusual one. Hair is considered to be powerful medicine. I could understand if an old man had that name. It's unusual for a boy."

I didn't confront Rachel with any of this new information I had come across. It sounded too absurd. I didn't really believe it myself, anyway. Yet it kept coming into my head, and particularly when I looked into the black, piercing eyes of the boy, I felt a strange and eerie sensation. Over the next few weeks, I tried to put all thoughts of witchcraft out of my mind. I concentrated on my work. Water Dog had not been around to bother me, but I did continue to carry my pistol when I went out of the house.

It was mid-December, and a light snow had fallen. I was sitting in my easy chair with a cup of coffee when I realized that it had been dark for some time and the boy had not come in. I got up and went to the front door.

"Where are you going?" asked Rachel.

"I'm just going to check on that boy," I said. "He should be inside by now."

I stepped outside and saw him right away. He was sprinkling something across the road just down from the house. "What are you doing out there?" I said.

He turned and looked at me, and even in the darkness, I fancied that I could see those eyes fixing on me. He didn't speak.

"Come on in the house," I said. "It looks as if we might get a little storm tonight." There were a few distant and low rumbles of thunder to be heard now and then.

"It's just the Thunder Boys," said Round Hair.

"I want you to come inside," I said, raising my voice. I was exasperated with him. I'd had all I wanted of his ignoring my wishes. I started toward him with the intent of dragging him into the house, when a sudden streak of lightning sliced into a small tree that stood just on the near side of the line he had drawn in the road. The sound of the tree splitting was joined by a sudden clap of thunder, and I was thrown to the ground on my back. The tree toppled sideways to lie along the ditch beside the road and left standing only a small piece of trunk about three feet tall. When I recovered my senses, I stood up. I started to say something to the boy, changed my mind, and turned to go into the house.

Rachel was standing in the doorway. "Are you all right?" she said.

"Yes."

I brushed past her and went inside, still as much shaken by my anger at the boy as by the fright I had received.

"Come on in now," Rachel called out into the night.

"Okay."

And Round Hair came inside.

The next day was Sunday, and I was glad to have a day off work. I was at the table finishing my breakfast when I heard the sound of horse hooves out on the road. The boy had gone out the front door just a few minutes before. Rachel went to the door and opened it to look out. "It's Water Dog," she said.

I ran to stand beside her. He had stopped his horse a little ways down the road and was looking toward our house. Suddenly he shouted. "Hey!" he said. "Rachel! Send your new man out here. I'm going to kill him."

"By god," I said, "this has gone far enough." I went to get my pistol.

"Stay here," said Rachel.

"Not this time," I said, and I pushed her aside so I could go through the door. Round Hair had gone out into the road and stood staring at his father. The man ignored him and watched me walk into the yard. He laughed and kicked his horse in the sides. I was only halfway to the road when Water Dog, racing his mount, reached the line that Round Hair had sprinkled onto the road the night before, and the animal shied. Water Dog kicked it and lashed at it with the quirt he carried, but to no avail. The horse screamed, in terror, I thought, and reared up high on its hind legs. Round Hair stood calmly in front of it, as if he knew that it would not run over him. When the horse finally brought its forelegs back down to earth, it began to buck. Suddenly Water Dog was thrown. He flew high into the air, and when he came down, the small of his back met the jagged tree stump left by the lightning. The force of his fall rammed the stump completely through his body at such an angle that it tore through his crotch in the front.

"My god," I said. "I'll go for a doctor."

"No," said Rachel. "He'll bleed to death soon. Let him."

Round Hair, his expression the same as always, looked at the man who had been his father, then slowly turned his black eyes toward his mother. I stood apart with the strange feeling that I was not even involved in their scene.

A SHORT RADIO PLAY FROM
JAMES MOONEY

Brass

NARRATOR: A boy lived with his mother outside of town, because he had sores all over his body and did not want anyone to see him. He had never known his father. One day his mother spoke to him.

MOTHER: Son, perhaps I should have told you sooner. Your father is a great doctor. He lives far to the west, but if you can find him, he can cure you of those spots. He is Thunder.

BOY: Thunder! How can that be?

MOTHER: He sometimes comes to earth, and one time he came down and came all the way out here to the east. You were born after that. He is your father.

BOY: Mother, if you will prepare me some food for the journey, I will go ahead and find him.

NARRATOR: The boy traveled to the west, and at every house he came to, he stopped.

BOY: Do you know where Thunder lives?

A MAN: He lives far to the west.

NARRATOR: The boy traveled on and on. At another house:

BOY: Do you know where Thunder lives?

A MAN: To the west, but it's not far.

NARRATOR: And at another:

BOY: Can you tell me the way to the house of Thunder?

BRASS: Oh, he's not far from here, but come and play a game with me.

BOY: I don't have time. I must find Thunder.

BRASS: You can play a game with me first. It's a game of my own invention. I call it *gatayusti*. We play it with a stone and a stick, and we can bet on who will win.

BOY: I have nothing to bet.

BRASS: (*Laughs*) We can play for your pretty spots. Come on.

BOY: I tell you, I have no time. I've traveled a long distance looking for Thunder. He's my father, and I must find him.

BRASS: He just lives in the next house, so you have time. We can play a game or two.

BOY: I have to go find my father first, but I will stop and play with you on my way back.

NARRATOR: At Thunder's home, someone came to tell him the news.

MESSENGER: Thunder, there is a boy traveling this direction looking for you. He says that he's your son.

THUNDER: I have traveled far and wide, and I have many children. On the other hand, anyone would want to be my child. Bring him here, and we'll find out.

NARRATOR: So the boy was brought to Thunder and shown the way in. Thunder showed the boy a chair and told him to sit down. The chair was covered by a blanket, but Thunder did not tell the boy that under the blanket the chair was made from a honey locust tree and the sharp thorns were sticking up. The boy sat down and was not hurt.

THUNDER: (*Aside*) This must indeed be my son. (*Aloud*) Why have you come to see me?

BOY: I have sores all over my body, and my mother told me you were my father and a great doctor, and if I came here you would cure me.

THUNDER: Yes. (*Puffing up*) I am a great doctor. I'll soon fix you. Wife!

THUNDER'S WIFE: Yes.

THUNDER: Take that huge pot and fill it with water and put it over the fire.

NARRATOR: In a few moments the water was boiling, and Thunder put some roots in it. Then he picked up the boy, lifted him over the pot, and dropped him into the boiling water. But the boy was not hurt.

THUNDER: Wife, take the pot and throw it in the river, boy and all.

NARRATOR: The wife did as she was told, and when the pot with the boiling water went into the river, an eddy was created. There was a service tree and a calico bush growing on the bank above, and a great cloud of steam rose up and created streaks and blotches on their bark. When the steam cleared, the boy was seen clinging to the roots of the service tree. His skin was clear.

THUNDER'S WIFE: Here, take my hand and climb out. We'll walk together to the house. When we get back to the house, your father will offer you some new dress. When he opens his box and tells you to select your ornaments, reach all the way to the bottom. Then he will send for his other sons to play ball with you. There is a honey locust tree in front of the house. When you get tired, strike at that, for it is his favorite tree, and he doesn't want anything to happen to it.

THUNDER: Ah, I knew I could cure those spots. Now we must dress you. Put on those new buckskins. This belt. This headdress. That looks good. Now get your necklace and bracelets out of this box.

NARRATOR: Thunder opened the box, and the boy looked in. It was filled with snakes all gliding over each other. The boy remembered what Thunder's wife had told him, and he plunged his hand into the mess of snakes all the way to the bottom of the box and pulled out a great rattlesnake, which he wrapped around his neck for a necklace. He reached down into the box four more times, and each time he pulled out a copperhead. He twisted them around his wrists and ankles.

THUNDER: Here, take this war club. Now you must play a ball game with your two elder brothers. They live in the Darkening Land beyond here, but I have sent for them.

NARRATOR: The young men came, and they were older and bigger than the boy, but he was not afraid, and he fought against them. All the time they played, thunder rolled and lightning flashed, for the two young men were the Little Thunders and the boy was Lightning. When Lightning grew tired, he aimed a blow at the honey locust tree.

THUNDER: Stop the game. It's done. Now, my son, I suppose you will go back home to your mother?

LIGHTNING: On my way here, Father, I stopped at the home of a man who called himself Brass. He tried to make me play a game with him. He called it *gatayusti*. To get away from him, I promised I would stop on the way home and play with him.

THUNDER: Hmm. Yes, I know him. He is a great gambler. He makes his living that way. But I will see that you win. Take this gourd and tie it to your waist. Inside the gourd is a string of beads. You see the one end hanging out of this hole in the top? Inside the gourd there is no end to the string. Now, go on back the way you came. He will want to play you for these beads. This time he will lose every game. When he cries out for a drink, you will know he's getting tired. Then strike the rock with your war club, and water will come out. At last he will bet his life and lose. Then call your brothers to come and kill him, for he is tricky, and he will cheat and get away.

NARRATOR: The boy returned to the home of Brass with his gourd and his war club.

BRASS: Ahh, you've come back, and this time you have something to bet, I see.

NARRATOR: The boy pulled out a string until it encircled the playing ground.

LIGHTNING: I'll play this much for one game against your bet.

BRASS: I'll win your beads. No one can beat me.

NARRATOR: They played a game, and the boy won.

BRASS: I don't understand it. Let's play again.

NARRATOR: They played again, and the boy won again. They played away half the day.

BRASS: It's a very hot day. I want to get a drink.

LIGHTNING: No, we'll keep playing.

NARRATOR: He struck the rock with his war club, and water came out for them to drink.

BRASS: I have nothing left to bet except my wife. We'll play for her.

NARRATOR: The boy pulled out more string from his gourd for a bet, and they played, and the boy won.

BRASS: Another game! Another game!

LIGHTNING: But you have nothing left to bet.

BRASS: We'll play another game. If I win, I can kill you, but if you win, you can kill me.

LIGHTNING: All right, let's play.

NARRATOR: They played another game, and the boy won again.

BRASS: Before you kill me, let me go and tell my wife. Then you can kill me.

NARRATOR: Brass went into the house, but he did not come back out. Lightning went into the house to see what was keeping Brass, but he found that the house had a back door, and Brass had gone out that way. He ran back to Thunder's house and got his brothers. The Thunder Boys brought their dog, the Green Horned Beetle, and they all hurried after Brass. They came across an old woman making pottery.

LIGHTNING: Have you seen Brass come by here?

OLD WOMAN: No, I have not.

1st THUNDER BOY: He came this way.

OLD WOMAN: Then he must have passed in the night, for I have been here all day.

NARRATOR: A beetle was circling in the air above the old woman's head, and it suddenly made a dive at her. It struck her on the forehead, and it made a sound like the ringing of brass. Then they knew it was Brass, and they sprang at him, but quick as a flash, he jumped up in his right shape and ran off. He was soon out of sight. The beetle had a little brass color rubbed off on its forehead. They ran after Brass, and they came across an old man carving a stone pipe.

2nd THUNDER BOY: Have you seen Brass come by this way?

OLD MAN: No one has come by here.

NARRATOR: The beetle struck the old man on the forehead, and it rang like metal. But Brass jumped up again in his right form and ran away fast. The brothers and the beetle chased Brass until he ran out of breath and could go no further. He had reached the edge of the world at the great water where the sun goes down. They tied his hands and feet with a grapevine, and then they ran a long pole through his breast and planted it out in the water. They put two crows on top of the pole to guard it. But Brass never died. He cannot die until the end of the world. He just lies there, always with his face up. Sometimes he struggles to get free, and sometimes the beavers, his friends, gnaw at the grapevines, but when they do that, the pole shakes, and the crows at the top cry out and frighten the beavers away.

SOUND OF CROWS: Ka! Ka! Ka!

THE COWBOY WESTERNS

The Execution

Joe Harman was sixty years old. He knew that he really ought to retire. He'd been in the law enforcement business for forty years, more or less, having started out in the old days as a deputy for old Bill Neeley in Texas. Bill had been dead for nigh onto eighteen years now. He was shot in the back by a drunken cowboy in McAllen late one night. Joe had already moved on by that time, but he heard about it not long afterward. He was working for Sheriff Dode Johnson then. Dode himself bought the farm about a year after that. He was riding with a posse on the trail of some two-bit bank robbers. The outlaws laid an ambush, and poor old Dode was the first one to fall dead. The posse killed all the outlaws, but when they hauled the bodies in, Dode's was one of them.

Joe forced himself to think about something else. Looking back over the years, he could catalogue all the lawmen, city marshals, county sheriffs, even a U.S. marshal once, that he had worked for, and he could recite the manner of each of their deaths. None had lived to a ripe old age. None had died peacefully. Joe counted himself lucky to have lived so long, and to still be working. But on that last point, he still thought that it was about time he quit. He really ought to take off his badge, hang up his guns, and stop pushing his luck.

Maybe when this business with the Kid was over, he would do just that. The Kid was Marion Somerville. No one could blame him for wanting to be called the Kid, and no one had dared to call him Marion or laugh about his name for some time, not since those first two he killed. The first one was in the saloon in Joe's town, but the Kid managed to prod the unfortunate bastard into going for his gun first. Joe had no choice. All the witnesses called it the same way: self-defense. The next one was more questionable, but it happened somewhere else, outside of Joe's jurisdiction. At any rate, ever since then, everyone had called Marion Somerville the Kid. There had been no more trouble, not on that score.

The Kid really had been just a kid when Joe had first taken the job as town marshal. He was maybe twelve years old, although he looked more like nine or ten because he was so scrawny. He had been in and out of trouble the whole time he was growing up. His folks were poor. The old man couldn't quite seem to make a living. The mother looked like she was always just a step away from the grave. Then when the Kid was maybe sixteen years old, the old man skipped out on them. The mother didn't last long after that.

No one bothered about the Kid. He probably should have been taken into custody by the state and had a home hunted up for him. But he stayed in the shack he had grown up in, and he found himself a job in town, sweeping out the general store and running errands. His first payday, he bought himself a Colt .45. It was used, but it was in good shape. It took all of his pay. He had to wait till his next payday to buy bullets, and then he started practicing. He spent all of his spare time with his Colt, shooting tin cans and bottles off of fence posts, practicing a fast draw, shooting at rabbits, squirrels, crows.

The Kid wasn't really all that bad. He'd had a rough time growing up. And he never did grow up much. He was still skinny and scrawny and not very tall, but he showed everyone around why the Colt was sometimes called the Equalizer, beginning that first day. He had recently bought a gun belt and holster, and he had practiced with it until he got comfortable drawing and firing. He had just turned eighteen, and he went into the saloon wearing his new gun belt and carrying his Colt. He walked up to the bar and ordered a shot of whiskey.

Sam King was standing at the bar. He laughed out loud. The Kid looked down the bar and saw Sam standing there alone and laughing. Joe was not there, but this is the way it was told to him later by all the witnesses.

"What's so funny?" the Kid asked.

"You really going to drink that whiskey, Marion?" asked King.

"I mean to drink it, if it's any of your business," the Kid said. "And don't call me that name."

"Marion? It's your name, ain't it? Ain't that what your maw had wrote down on the paper when you was born?"

"Never mind about that. Just call me Kid. That's all."

"Kid? Like in Billy the Kid? You ain't no Billy the Kid, but maybe we could call you Kid Marion. You like that all right? Kid Marion."

"I told you not to call me by that name."

Everyone else in the saloon got quiet. They were watching the business between the Kid and Sam King. It didn't quit, either. It heated up. Finally the Kid said, "I can make you shut up, you ugly son of a bitch."

King turned to face the Kid square. His intentions were clear. "Try it," he said.

"I'm waiting on you, you chicken shit," the Kid said.

King went for his gun, but the Kid was faster. No one had seen him in action before that day. One bullet killed Sam King. No one called the Kid Marion anymore after that, either, at least not at home. His second killing came somewhere out of town, and the word came back to them in secondhand stories. Joe never talked with any actual witness of that one. Some said the Kid had drawn first. Some said he shot a man in the back. As far as Joe Harman was concerned, whatever happened had taken place outside of his jurisdiction, and that was all there was to it. He had no curiosity beyond that.

But the Kid had quit his job, and he always seemed to have money. He also spent a great deal of time away from home. When he was away, people talked about him. They said he was out stealing cattle, or robbing banks, or murdering travelers for whatever valuables they had on them. Some were kinder. They said he was out working as a hired gunfighter. The only thing that was certain was that he was getting money from somewhere, and he was getting more and more cocky all the time.

Then came the day that had led directly up to the current situation. Joe had been laid up with a bad case of bronchitis for almost a week. He was in bed at the Widow Henshaw's boarding house, where he lived. His deputies Rance Hughes and Edgar Seabolt came by to see him.

"The Kid's back in town," Rance said.

"He's spoiling for a fight," Seabolt said.

Joe was tired, and he hurt. He didn't really want to be bothered with all this. He was more than a little grumpy when he responded. "If he starts a fight, arrest him. If someone else starts it, that's their hard luck. Just take care of it, boys. Leave me be."

Well, they took care of it, all right. Rance pulled the Kid's own tactics on him, goading him into a fight to the point of making him go for his gun first. The only problem for Rance was that the Kid was like greased lightning. Rance was killed with one shot. Seabolt, though, unbeknownst to the Kid, had been standing just behind him, and Rance's body had not even hit the floor before Seabolt brained the Kid with the barrel of his Merwin & Hulbert revolver. The Kid dropped like a sack of grain. When he woke up, he was sitting in a jail cell. Seabolt had charged him with the murder of Rance Hughes, a deputy marshal. All this had been reported to Joe Harman in his sickbed.

By the time the trial date came around, Joe was up and about again. He was still hacking some, but mostly he was recovered. He went into his office that first day he was up, and he saw the Kid sitting on the edge of the cot in the jail cell. He also saw Seabolt sitting in his chair behind his desk. Seabolt popped up and moved to the chair behind the smaller deputy's desk. Joe said nothing about it. He walked over to the stove and poured a cup of coffee. Then he walked to the cell.

"Coffee, Kid?" he asked.

The Kid looked up at him for a moment. Then he stood up and walked over to the bars, reaching for the cup. "Sure," he said. Joe went back to the stove and poured another cup. He moved back over to the cell.

"What'd you do it for, Kid?" he asked. "You've never been that stupid before."

"It was a setup, marshal," the Kid said. "I didn't see it then, but I can see it now. That Rance come up in front of me and went to prodding me. Seabolt there had slipped up behind me real quiet-like. The only thing is, neither one of the clumsy bastards was fast enough. I killed Rance. Then Seabolt hit me from behind."

"You went for your gun first," Joe said.

"Yeah, well, he made me mad. He was asking for it."

Joe shook his head. "Well," he said, "you'll have a trial, and the jury will make a decision, but I don't see any way you can beat this one, Kid. It looks bad for you."

Joe noticed over the next few days that Seabolt was bordering on mistreating the prisoner. He stopped just short of any real rough stuff, but if he had to take the Kid out back, he shoved him along the way, in spite of the fact that the Kid's ankles were shackled together. One time he shoved too hard, and the Kid fell down. Joe jumped up: "Seabolt, God damn it."

The Kid struggled to his feet, and Seabolt looked back at Joe and shrugged. "I didn't mean it," he said. "He's just so scrawny. He don't weigh hardly nothing."

"Well, you watch yourself," said Joe. "We can't be treating prisoners that way."

"The little shit killed Rance, Joe," Seabolt whined.

"And you're a lawman, you son of a bitch," said Joe. "You just mind what I tell you."

Joe thought that he should have fired Seabolt, but the timing just wasn't right. He'd had two deputies. One was dead. And he had a prisoner that could be dangerous. He had no one in mind to replace either deputy, the dead one or the live one, so he would just have to hang on to Seabolt until this thing was all over. Seabolt minded his manners for the most part when Joe was around, but Joe wondered how the man acted when he wasn't there.

One day, just before the trial, Joe walked into the office unexpectedly and caught Seabolt threatening the Kid with a cocked and loaded double-barreled shotgun. "Come on, Kid," Seabolt was saying. "Make a move at me, why don't you? You touch them bars, and I'll splatter you all over the back wall."

"What you gonna do after you splatter me?" the Kid asked. "Unlock the door? Tell Joe that I broke out somehow? You better make up a good story, you cocksucker. They'll hang you instead of me."

"We'll see about that, Marion," said Seabolt.

Joe decided that he'd heard enough. He stepped on into the office. "Seabolt," he snapped.

Seabolt looked over his shoulder, but he was loath to move the shotgun. He still held it pointed at the Kid.

"Seabolt," said Joe. "Put away that gun. Now."

Reluctantly, Seabolt lowered the shotgun and eased the hammers down. Joe took it out of his hands. "Now, get out of here," he said.

"Where'll I go?"

"Get something to eat. Go have a drink. I don't give a damn. Just get out of here."

The trial didn't last long. No one had expected it to. The jury found the Kid guilty of murder in the first degree, and the judge sentenced him to hang in exactly one week. There was no appeal. There would be no delay. Joe had to hire some carpenters to build a gallows.

Every day, the Kid stood at the window of his cell looking out on the progress of the construction. Every day inside the office, Seabolt made some comments about hanging. "It's an awful way to go," he said one day. "You ever see a man hang? His tongue pokes out, and his eyes bug out. Sometimes he shits his pants. I ain't never checked real close to be sure, but I heard they get a hard-on just when they drop. You ever hear the story of ole Black Jack Ketchum when they hung him? Snapped his head right off, they did. Snapped it right off. I seen pictures of it. The body laying over here with the hands still tied behind it, the head, still wearing the hood, laying over on this side. Course, I don't think you have to worry about that, Kid, you're so damn skinny you don't weigh hardly nothing."

"Seabolt, either shut up or get out," said Joe.

"Don't worry about him, Joe," said the Kid. "He ain't bothering me none."

But Joe knew that the Kid was lying to save face. He was acting tough. He had to. It was all that was left for him, to go to the gallows like a man, to show no fear, to die game. That was all he had.

At last the appointed day came around. The gallows had been finished and the trapdoor tested over and over again. Everything was ready. Joe told Seabolt to unlock the cell door, and the Kid stood up, ready to go, working hard at appearing unconcerned. Joe thought that he looked like a scared kid who was about to take a licking at school for having dipped a little girl's pigtails in the inkwell. As the Kid stepped out of the cell, Seabolt gave him a shove.

Joe grabbed Seabolt's shirt front and looked him hard in the eyes. "Seabolt, I'm warning you for the last time," he said as they began the short walk to the waiting gallows. A crowd had gathered in the streets, curious to watch a man die by hanging. The noose dangled. The Kid hesitated as they stepped out through the door of the jailhouse. Then he took a deep breath, pulling himself up as tall as he could, and he led the way to the gallows and up the steps. Joe and Seabolt were a step behind him, one to his right, the other to his left. On top, they placed him carefully on the trapdoor, and Joe read the death sentence. He asked if the Kid had anything to say before the sentence was executed, and the Kid said, "Hell, no. Get it over with."

Seabolt put a black bag over the Kid's head, and then he placed the noose. Joe checked it to make sure everything was all right. The man at the lever looked at Joe, and Joe nodded, but just as he did so, in that split instant between his nod and the actual releasing of the trapdoor, he had a horrible and panicked thought. He looked up quickly as the Kid plunged through the opening, and he could see that the rope was short. It had very little slack. The kid did not drop far. He did not weigh much. His neck did not break. Instead, he hung there, slowly strangling as his skinny body twisted at the end of the rope.

The crowd was gasping and whispering to one another. On the other side of the gallows platform, Seabolt was grinning. There was nothing that Joe could do. The execution was in progress, and it was according to law. He had to wait. He had to let the Kid gag to death slowly, his head in the darkness of the black hood, his body spinning. The horrors the Kid was suffering, both physical and mental, were unimaginable. It seemed like ten minutes before the body hung limp, before the Kid was dead, before it was all over at last.

Joe walked into his office feeling sick. He left the details of the cleanup to others. He had waited way too long to retire. He shouldn't even have been there. He thought again of the long list of lawmen he had worked for and worked with whose short lives had come to violent ends. God, he needed a drink. He walked back out of the office and headed for the saloon. Seabolt caught up with him on the sidewalk and fell in step.

"Well, we got that over with," Seabolt said.

"You're fired," said Joe.

"What?"

"You heard me right. You're fired."

Joe turned into the saloon and stopped at the bar, ordering a whiskey. The bartender turned to fetch it, and Seabolt sidled up to Joe.

"What for?" he said.

"I don't have to tell you," Joe said. "You wouldn't understand if I did. Just stay out of my way, that's all."

He wondered if his replacement would give the sorry son of a bitch his job back. He hoped not. He meant to announce to the town council in a short while his intention to retire. He figured he'd have to stay on long enough for them to find a replacement for him, but he hoped that wouldn't take long.

"Hey," Seabolt said, "you can't fire me. I ain't done nothing to get fired for."

"Get out of my face," Joe said as the barkeep put a shot glass and a bottle on the bar in front of him. Joe dug a coin out of a pocket and tossed it on the bar. The bartender poured whiskey into the shot glass.

"You hear what I said?" said Seabolt. "I didn't do nothing to get fired for."

Joe lifted the glass and took a sip, and the feeling it gave him was comforting, almost satisfying, but not quite. "You listening to me?" Seabolt shouted into the side of Joe's head.

"Get out of here, Seabolt," said Joe.

There were different stories told about what happened next. Some said that Seabolt pulled out his gun as he reached up with his other hand to spin Joe around. Others said that he only took hold of Joe's shoulders to force Joe to look him in the eyes. All of that would have to come out at the trial. A jury would have to decide. Everyone agreed, though, that Joe Harman's gun was out in a flash, that he fired once, so close to Seabolt's belly that the shirt caught fire, that Seabolt fell but did not die instantly. He lay on the floor looking up with puzzled eyes at his killer for maybe ten full minutes before he breathed his last.

Nate's Revenge

Nate Crowley stepped out of the stage into the main street of Tombstone. It was a busy street, crowded and loud with traffic. He had read about Tombstone. He knew that it was a busy town because of the silver mining, but he was still surprised at the bustle and the bluster. His one small bag landed at his feet and stirred up a cloud of dust. He bent to pick it up, looked around for a likely place to sleep, then headed for the nearest rooming house. He didn't stay long in the room, just long enough to deposit his bag. He left again, headed for the nearest saloon.

Nate thought that all eyes would be on him as he headed into the booze hall. He was a stranger. He was a snappy dresser, in a smart three piece-suit, and he was nearly six feet tall. But as he stepped into the crowded establishment, he was surprised that no one even seemed to notice him. He couldn't decide whether he was relieved or disappointed. His common sense told him that it was best this way. He didn't really want to call attention to himself. He walked to the bar and ordered a whiskey.

He was pleased to note that he could keep his back to the room and, leaning on the bar, could study a large part of the big room in the long mirror behind the bar. He wanted to get a look at all the faces if he could, but he wanted to do so without calling any attention to himself. He sipped his whiskey, because he wanted to keep a clear head. He had only ordered the drink so no one would question his presence in the saloon.

He was looking for Ira Long. He had good reason to believe that Ira would be in Tombstone, and he had endured a long, expensive, and uncomfortable trip for just that reason. It had been seven years since he had seen Ira, and he hoped that he would recognize Ira before Ira saw and recognized him. He meant for all the surprise to be on Ira's side. He meant to kill Ira. It was almost all he had thought about for these last seven years. It was all he had lived for. It meant everything to him.

As he sipped his whiskey, Nate glanced from one face to another in the mirror. None were familiar. But he knew that somewhere in this town he would find Ira. His mind wandered back to that time seven years ago, that time that had changed his entire life, that time when he and Ira had been the best of friends. In those days, Nate would gladly have laid down his life for his friend. He very nearly had. He had given five years, but in the process, he had also learned that Ira's view of friendship was very different from his own.

They had been fun-loving young men, more than a bit wild. They had met punching cows on a ranch in New Mexico, and they had hit it off at once. Both young men liked drinking, chasing women, a good fistfight, and shooting. There was no malice in it, just good, clean fun. They were a little rowdy, Nate admitted to himself, but then so were most of the cowboys he knew, and none of them meant any harm, and for the most part no one ever got hurt, at least not badly.

But then there had come a time when the punchers' pay just didn't go far enough for the two fun-loving cowboys. There was never enough money for the fun they pursued. They tried gambling, but they lost more than they won, and that made their problem even worse than it had been before. The whiskey and the women cost money. So did the bullets. The only thing they enjoyed that was free was a fistfight. They had to do something. They talked it over and decided on a life of crime.

Their first job was a stagecoach holdup. It netted them a few dollars, and they decided that it had hardly been worth the risk. So they robbed a store. That wasn't much better. They decided they would rob banks, and for a while they got away with it. They had more money than they could spend, but their identities became known, and they had to hit the trail.

They had a few thousand dollars with them, all in Nate's saddlebags, when the posse got on their trail. The lawmen had slipped up on them somehow. Even seven years later, Nate was more than a little embarrassed about that fact. He and Ira should have noticed such a large posse sooner. So many men and horses should not have gotten so close to them without some kind of warning. But they had, and the two partners in crime had mounted up to run for it. The posse had been close behind, close enough for some of the men to start shooting from the saddle as they rode.

It's a tough thing to get off a good shot while riding on the back of a running horse, but one of the lawmen's shots got Ira's horse and sent Ira sprawling in the trail. Nate reined in his mount and looked back. There was Ira in the dirt, and not far behind him the posse was closing the gap fast. It was crazy to think of going back for Ira. It was crazy to think of trying to outrun them with two men on a horse. But Ira was his partner, and Nate didn't think. He only reacted. He rode back, reached down, and helped Ira onto the back of his horse. Bullets from the fast-approaching posse whizzed past them as Nate whipped up the horse again. Ira looked over his shoulder.

"They're catching up, Nate," he shouted. "It's all over for us."

"Shut up," Nate yelled back. "We'll get out of this together, or we'll go down together. Sling some lead in their direction. That might slow them down."

Ira slipped his six-gun out of his holster. "Sorry, Nate," he said, "but this riding double will never do." He banged the barrel of his revolver down on Nate's head. It struck only a glancing blow, but it was painful nonetheless, and dizzying. Nate struggled with the fuzziness in his head from the surprising blow and from the even more surprising source of the blow. Then Ira hit him again and pushed him from the saddle. Nate hit the road hard, bouncing and rolling. The next thing he knew, he was being manhandled by members of the posse. Ira was long gone—with Nate's horse and with all the money.

Five years in prison had followed for Nate. It had taken two more years for him to get a little money together and to get some word of Ira's whereabouts. Those seven years had seemed like a lifetime to Nate, but at last they were over. The source of his information was good. He trusted it absolutely. He knew that Ira was in Tombstone, and he knew that he would see him soon. Then he would even the score. It wasn't just that someone had knocked him in the head and stolen his horse and all of his money. It wasn't just that someone had let him take the rap and had gotten away clean. It was that *Ira* had done all these things to him. Ira, his best friend, his partner, had done all that, and he had done it after Nate had endangered himself by going back to help him. If it had been someone else, it wouldn't have mattered all that much. But it had been Ira, and there was no forgetting or forgiving that.

Nate took another sip of his whiskey, and he noticed that the bartender shot him a glance. It occurred to him that he might be irritating the bartender by drinking so slowly, but he had no intention of gulping the stuff. He continued searching the crowd, studying the faces in the mirror. He saw nothing familiar in any of them. The far side of the room to his right was beyond his vision in the reflection, so, having scrutinized all he could by looking over the bar, he turned casually, his drink in his right hand, his left elbow resting on the bar, and he looked toward that end of the room. There was no sign of Ira. Leaving half his drink in the glass, he left the saloon.

He hit four more saloons using the same technique and with the same results. He thought that he could spend a month just casing the saloons in Tombstone. He had never seen a town with so many such establishments. It was hard for him to believe, even with the busy streets, that one town could support so many. It was a tedious job he had given himself, but he could think of no other way to locate Ira. Even though he was sipping his drinks and not finishing them, he was beginning to feel the effects of the alcohol. His capacity for booze had diminished considerably during his five years in prison, and in the two years following, he had not managed to regain it. He went to his room to sleep.

Nate's sleep was troubled and fitful that night. It was filled with images of Ira. Some of the images were pleasant. They were images of the early days, the days when the two young men had been inseparable friends, happy and carefree, drinking, chasing women, brawling in the saloons, robbing stagecoaches, banks, and country stores, and spending money lavishly and wildly. Then they changed to the time when Ira had betrayed him. They were riding double on Nate's horse, the posse close behind. Ira pounded Nate on the head with his pistol and threw him off the racing horse. He landed hard, bounced, and rolled, over and over again.

Then the dreams changed again. They became hopeful dreams of the future, dreams in which Nate faced a frightened Ira, and Ira dropped to his knees to beg forgiveness, to plead for his life. Nate was hard and unmoving. He drew his revolver, thumbed back the hammer, and pointed the barrel at Ira's chest. Ira cried and whimpered. Nate smiled. His finger tightened on the trigger, and he woke up in a cold sweat, only to sleep again and dream again.

The following morning, Nate got up and dressed. He left his sidearm and holster in the room and placed a British Webley Bulldog in his right jacket pocket. He didn't want to appear to be a gunfighter or even someone looking for a fight, but he did want to be ready in case he ran across his prey. He went out to find himself some breakfast. In the street and over his meal, he studied the faces of everyone he saw. There was still no sign of Ira. He decided that he would have to change his tactics and start to ask questions. He had hoped to be able to just spot Ira. Asking around could backfire on him. Someone might get the word back to Ira that he was being looked for. Still, it was better than what he had been doing. He could watch and wait until all his money was spent and still not achieve his goal.

He walked over to the Oriental Saloon. He hadn't yet gone into the Oriental. Even so, he was not going there to do what he had been doing in the other saloons. He was going to ask questions. Inside, the place was not too crowded, for it was early in the day. He went directly to the bar and leaned his elbows on it.

The bartender, not busy, came right over. "What can I do for you?" he asked.

"Can I get a cup of coffee?" Nate asked.

"Sure."

The bartender turned away to get the coffee, and when he brought it back and placed it in front of Nate, Nate tossed a coin on the bar. "Say," he said, "I'm looking for someone. An old friend of mine. Used to be my partner. I heard he was here in Tombstone, but I ain't had no luck spotting him around town. Maybe you know him. Name's Ira Long."

The bartender shook his head. "Never heard of him," he said. "Sorry."

"Well," Nate said, "there's a lot of folks in this town."

"More come in every day," the bartender said. "It's the silver mines. It brings in prospectors, gamblers, entertainers, drummers, all kinds. You might check with the marshal. Him and his brothers try to keep up with everything that goes on around here."

"Thanks," Nate said. "Where's his office?"

"It's right down the street," the bartender said, "but he's sitting right over there." He gave a nod. "That's him, Virgil Earp, and that's his brother Wyatt with him."

Nate took another slurp of his coffee and put the cup down. "Thanks again," he said. He walked over to the table the bartender had indicated and found two men with handlebar mustaches wearing black suits and visiting over coffee.

"Excuse me," he said. "Marshal Earp?"

The two Earp brothers looked up at Nate. "That's me," said Virgil. "What can I do for you?"

"My name's Nate Crowley," Nate said. "I just got into town yesterday on the stage. I'm looking for an old friend, a partner of mine, name of Ira Long. I heard he was in town, and I come looking for him. I ain't seen him in seven years, and I come a long ways to find him. He was the best friend I ever had. The bartender said that if anyone would know about him, it would likely be you."

"What name did you say?" Virgil asked.

"Ira Long," said Nate.

Virgil shook his head and looked at Wyatt.

"Never heard of him," Wyatt said. "What's he look like?"

"About my size and age," Nate said. "But he's got blond hair and blue eyes. Pretty good-looking fellow. He used to get all the best-looking gals when we was running together. He's a little bowlegged, I reckon. Worked as a cowboy for a lot of years. Both of us did."

"Well, I wish we could help you," Virgil said, "but that don't call anyone to mind. Course, there's a bunch of folks in Tombstone who come to town with new names. Could be your partner's like that, not using his right name anymore."

Nate hadn't thought of that, but it made good sense. Ira was still wanted for his part in the old robberies, and he would likely have a pretty good idea that Nate would be looking for him sooner or later. Probably Marshal Earp was right. Probably Ira wasn't using his own real name here in Tombstone. This was going to be even tougher than Nate had thought.

"You might check the claims office," Wyatt said, "and the real estate offices. If he came to mine or if he got himself any property, they'd know about him. Course, they won't be any help if he's using a different name."

"Thanks," Nate said. "I reckon it'll be worth a try."

Nate left the saloon and started on the rounds suggested by Wyatt Earp. He had no luck in the claims office or the first two real estate offices. He was in the third realty office, feeling like this too was a waste of time, but when he gave the man a description of Ira, the man scratched his head and wrinkled his brow in thought.

"Well, sir," he said, "I sure don't know any Ira Long, but the description sounds like it could be Mr. Thomas."

"Mr. Thomas?" Nate said, suddenly excited with hope.

"Mr. Richard Thomas," the man said. "You say it's been seven years since you saw your friend?"

"That's right," Nate said.

"Well, Mr. Thomas has been in Tombstone for nearly that long, I'd say. He come to town and bought himself a business. Been doing right well, he has. Dry goods store right down the street. You can't miss it. Got his name right out front on the sign: Thomas Dry Goods. Course, he might not be your friend at all, but he fits the description, all right. I can't think of anyone else."

"Thanks, mister," Nate said. "Thanks a lot."

Sure enough, Thomas Dry Goods was easy to find. Nate stood on the board sidewalk for a while, just studying the outside of the building. It had a facade like most of the other buildings on the street, and it had two large glass windows, each decorated with a variety of goods that were available inside. Up above the door and windows was a large sign with big red letters that identified the place as Thomas Dry Goods.

Old Ira's done right well for himself, Nate thought. Most likely he used the money from our last job to set himself up.

Nate was seething inside. He burned with a desire to confront Ira, to upbraid him for his cowardly act, and then to blast him to Kingdom Come. But how should he proceed? He couldn't just walk into the store and kill Ira then and there in cold blood. Surely he would not be able to escape the Earps and the sheriff, Johnny Behan. And likely Ira had new friends in this town. He had been here nearly seven years according to the real estate man. Nate thought that perhaps he could go inside and let Ira see him. Let Ira sweat it out. Maybe he could face Ira and challenge him to a fair gunfight. That way it wouldn't be called a murder. He had thought about this moment for so many years that now that it was nigh, he couldn't decide just how to proceed.

Then he reminded himself that it might not even be Ira in there. It was someone the people in town knew as Richard Thomas—a storekeeper. After all, maybe Richard Thomas was really Richard Thomas, and not Ira at all. Maybe he just happened to fit the general description that Nate had given of Ira. And it was difficult to imagine Ira as a storekeeper. Nate thought about going back to the Oriental and asking the Earps about Richard Thomas. They might know if the man was really who he said he was. But then that would be too obvious. They would want to know, if Nate's story was true, why he hadn't just gone into the store to see the man. At last he decided there was nothing to do but go inside and see for himself. He hitched his britches and walked to the door. Taking a deep breath, he opened the door and stepped inside.

There were four customers in the store, looking around at various items. A woman carried a bolt of cloth to the counter, where the clerk, also a woman, wrapped it up and collected the price from the customer. Nate looked at the woman behind the counter. She was young and beautiful. When she was no longer occupied, he walked over to the counter.

"May I help you, sir?" she asked.

"Well, yes, ma'am," Nate said, pulling his hat from his head. "I'm looking for the owner, Mr. Thomas."

"He isn't in just now," the woman said. "Perhaps I can help you. I'm Mrs. Thomas."

Nate was stunned. He hadn't expected this. Ira had a wife. If Thomas was really Ira. "No, thank you, ma'am," he said. "I really need to see Mr. Thomas. When do you expect him to be back?"

"He should be here around one o'clock," she said. "May I tell him who called?"

Nate hesitated a moment. "Oh, no, ma'am," he said. "I'll just drop back by later."

It seemed to Nate like the longest morning of his life. Mr. Thomas might not be Ira, but then again, he might be. And if he was, Nate was very close to him after these seven long years, seven years of hate and anticipation and longing for revenge. He tried to imagine the moment he would confront Mr. Thomas and discover him to actually be Ira. His mind constructed a conversation, the things he would say to Ira and Ira's response. He tried to picture the expression on Ira's face when Ira recognized him, the surprise, shock, fear.

He thought about the moment when he would pull the trigger, and he tried to imagine the expression of horror on Ira's face as the hot lead tore into his chest. And then his mind replayed the images from his dreams the night before. Then he wondered where Ira—or Mr. Thomas—might be, since he was not at his store. Would he be at home? He considered going back to the store to ask Mrs. Thomas where he could find her husband. But he discarded that idea. He should have asked while he was there in the store. He would feel foolish going back now to ask.

Considering it, though, put his mind back on the young woman in the store, Mrs. Thomas. If Ira really was Mr. Thomas, then that lovely young thing was his wife. A new image came into Nate's mind, a picture of the woman screaming in horror at the sight of her bloody, dying husband. He wondered whether Mr. Thomas, or Ira, had brought her with him when he arrived in Tombstone nearly seven years ago, or had he met her and married her in Tombstone? How long had they been married? Were there children? His mind was starting to feel sorry for the woman, but he steeled it against her. It was too bad that she had made such a sorry choice for a husband, a cowardly bastard who would steal a horse and money from his own partner, his best friend, even after that friend had put himself at risk to go back and rescue him from a fast-approaching posse.

No, he told himself. It was too bad about the little lady, but she didn't change anything. Ira had done what he had done, and it was a thing that could not be forgiven. It was a thing that he must pay for, and Nate intended to make him pay in full. That thought was all that had kept him going for the last seven years. It had to be done, and that's all there was to it. It had to be done, and Nate was going to do it. He only had to wait until one o'clock. After having waited for seven long years, he could wait until one o'clock.

Ira Long, in his new identity as Richard Thomas, respected Tombstone merchant, arrived at the store a little early. His wife was busy behind the counter with a customer, so Ira walked around behind the counter without a word. In another moment, the customer had been taken care of and was on her way out of the store. Ira stepped over to his wife and kissed her on the cheek. "You're early," she said.

"A little," Ira said. "The buggy's outside. You can go on home, sweetheart. I'll take over from here. Have you had a good morning?"

"Yes," she said. "Business has been brisk."

"Good," Ira said. "Well, now, you run on along home. I'll see you right after closing time."

She headed for the front door, but just before she opened it to go out, she paused and looked back over her shoulder at her husband. "Oh, Richard," she said, "there was a gentleman here earlier looking for you. He said he'd stop back by after one o'clock."

"What's his name?" Ira asked.

"He didn't say," she answered. "When I asked him, he just said that he'd stop back later. He was a nice-looking young man, and he was very polite. Well dressed."

"And he didn't say what his business was?"

"No, he didn't."

"Ah, well," said Ira. "I'll find out when he gets here. Don't worry about it. I'll see you for supper."

But when she had gone outside and shut the door, Ira's brow wrinkled. Who could be coming to see him, and what was his business? Why hadn't the man given his name? What could be so mysterious? Only one possibility came to his mind, and it was the one that had been plaguing him for seven years, ever since he had clubbed his partner Nate and left him to face the posse alone. It was a cowardly act, but it was an impulsive thing, based on an instinct for survival. As soon as he did it, he felt terrible pangs of guilt, and in seven years' time, they had not left him.

Many times over the years, he had thought that he should try to make things right with Nate, but really, there was no way that could be done. While Nate had been languishing in prison, Ira could not have done anything to get him out. He could only have gotten himself thrown in, and that wouldn't have helped Nate. As time passed, Ira accepted that he had been a coward and that he had betrayed his best friend. He decided that he would simply have to live with the terrible truth about himself and with the guilt that tormented him. And over the years, he had learned that he could live with it. It was a dark secret that he shared with no one, but he could live with it.

But that wasn't all. There was the fear. He had known all along that there was more than a chance that Nate would search him out. He had asked himself more than once, What would I have done had Nate done that to me? And the answer had always been the same: I would find him and kill him if it took the rest of my life. Nate had almost surely gone to jail, for the posse was practically on their heels when Ira dumped him off his horse. But for how long? They had done no killings, so it would not be forever. Sooner or later, Nate would be free again, and when that day came, Ira knew, Nate would be coming after him. He wouldn't know where to look, but he would be persistent. He would keep looking. And when Nate at last came, he would come looking to kill.

Ira didn't want to kill Nate. He felt guilty enough as things stood. But neither did he want to die. For now, especially, he had too much to lose. He had a lovely wife, with whom he was very much in love, and he had a good business. He still had a good many years of life left in him, unless his life should be cut short unnaturally. He didn't intend to let that happen if he could prevent it. He thought about closing the store, but then what would he tell his wife? And he couldn't just leave it closed indefinitely. If Nate knew where he was, he wouldn't leave town in a few days. He would wait around. Nate would have to come back to the store sooner or later. Then he thought about strapping on a six-gun, but he decided against that, too. He didn't think that Nate would be fool enough to gun down an unarmed man in the middle of the day in Tombstone.

Of course, he told himself, the man his wife had met earlier in the day might not even have been Nate. Maybe all this worry was for nothing. Even so, his heart jumped when the bell over the door jingled and a man wearing a gray suit stepped into the store. Ira looked at him hard, and when the man straightened up and looked toward him, Ira recognized him immediately, in spite of the changes of seven hard years. For a long and tense moment, the two men stood staring at one another. At last, Ira broke the uneasy silence.

"Hello, Nate," he said. "I thought it would be you. I knew you'd be coming for me sooner or later."

"I came to kill you, Ira," Nate said.

"I know," said Ira. He held his arms out to the side. "I'm not armed."

Nate held open his jacket. "Me neither," he said, although he lied, for the Webley was in his jacket pocket. "I thought we might just get reacquainted first. It's been a long time. The killing can wait. There's no hurry."

"You think that if you wait around long enough," Ira said, "I'll get nervous and make a try for you? Is that your game? Then when you kill me, you can call it self-defense."

Nate shrugged. "I don't know that I have any game," he said. "I just know that I've been looking for you for a long time, and I mean to kill you."

"I ain't going to just stand still for it," Ira said. "I know I done you wrong, and I feel bad about it. I've felt guilty about what I done all these years, but I'm not going to just let you kill me for it, no matter how guilty I feel."

"I figured you'd fight me," said Nate. "I wouldn't want it any other way, even though you don't deserve no better than a shot in the back with no warning."

"I won't argue with you, Nate," said Ira. "I agree that's what I deserve. Even so, like I told you, I won't just stand still for it. I won't just take it. I got too much to lose here, Nate. I got my wife and my business."

"A business, I reckon," said Nate, "that you got started using our money. Half of that money was mine."

"I'll give it to you, Nate," Ira said. "I've got it in the bank. I'll give you your share plus interest."

"If I just forget about what you done to me and ride out of here leaving you alive?"

"Yeah."

"I won't be bought off," Nate said. "I thought about this too many years."

The bell over the door jingled, and a customer came into the store. Nate moved over against the wall and sulked until the customer found what he was looking for, paid for it, and left. Then, "Shut her up," Nate said.

"What?" said Ira.

"Close the damn store," Nate said. "We don't need no more interruptions."

"If I close—"

Nate whipped the Webley out of his pocket and leveled it at Ira. "I said close it up," he snapped.

Slowly, Ira moved around the counter and over to the door. He flipped over the sign that said OPEN on one side and CLOSED on the other. Then he locked the door. He looked back at Nate. "You said you were unarmed," he said accusingly.

"I lied," said Nate. "Is that anywhere near as bad as what you done to me?"

"What now?" Ira asked.

"Well," said Nate, "I've changed my mind. I don't want to wait around. It's no fun. I think we ought to get the thing over with. You got a six-gun and a gun belt here?"

Ira nodded affirmatively.

"Is the gun loaded?"

"Yeah."

"Show me where it's at."

Ira indicated a location under the counter, and Nate moved around and pulled out the rig. He withdrew the revolver from its holster and examined it. It was fully loaded. "Okay," he said. "Wrap it up."

"Wrap it up?"

"You heard me," Nate snapped.

Ira wrapped the gun, belt, and holster as if it were a purchase. Nate picked it up off the counter and tucked it under his left arm. "All right," he said. "Let's go."

They walked to Nate's room, where Nate got his own revolver and belt. Then they walked to the livery stable, where he made Ira rent two saddle horses. They rode out of town together, neither man speaking. At last Nate stopped them. "This ought to do," he said. There was no one in sight in any direction. Both men dismounted, and Nate tossed the wrapped package to Ira. "Open it up and strap it on," he said.

Ira stood for a moment unbelieving. He held the package in front of him in both of his arms. He looked at Nate. "You mean to make this a fair fight?" he asked.

"A gun duel," Nate said.

"You said you came to kill me," said Ira.

"That's what I came for."

"In a fair fight," said Ira, "I might kill you. You think about that?"

"I was always faster than you," said Nate.

"But not as accurate," said Ira. "And you been a long time without practice."

"I been out of jail two years," said Nate. "I've had time to get back in shape. I'm better than I used to be. How about you, storekeeper? You been practicing?"

Ira stared at Nate, still unbelieving.

"Strap the damn thing on," snapped Nate.

Ira unwrapped the rig and wrapped the belt around his waist. "Go ahead," he said. "I won't draw on you. I can't."

"What the hell do you mean?" said Nate. "You beat me over the head and stole my horse and money. You left me for the damn posse. Left me to do five years in prison while you set yourself up as an honest, respectable storekeeper and got yourself a pretty wife. You did all that to me after I went back for you. You were down. I had my horse and I had the money. I had a good lead on that posse, too. But you went down, and I went back for you. After all that, you turned on me. And now you say you can't draw on me?"

"I won't," Ira said.

"You think that'll keep me from killing you?" Nate said. "Is that what you're trying to pull? You think I won't gun you down in cold blood? I will if you won't draw. If you won't go for your gun, I'll kill you anyway. I waited too many years for this. I come too far to find you."

Ira unbuckled the gun belt and let the rig fall to the ground at his feet. "Go ahead," he said. "Kill me. It won't give you back your lost years, and it won't give you back your share of the loot. But if it will ease your pain in any way, go ahead and shoot."

"Back in town," Nate said, "you told me you wouldn't stand still for this. Just what the hell are you trying to pull on me? You want to die? What about your store and your wife?"

"I thought about it all the way out here, Nate," said Ira. "We were best friends. We were partners. I put an end to all that by what I done, and it was a wrong thing for me to do. I never thought about it, Nate. I just done it, before I even knew what I was doing. It was like if a lion jumped up in my path, and I shot it real quick-like. You know what I mean? A reflex. There was no thought about it at all. I'm ashamed of it. I think about it every day. I dream about it. I'm living a lie. I won't add another wrong to what I done to you. I won't take a chance that I might win this fight. You might as well just go ahead and get it over with. Once you've killed me, you can strap that belt back on me. You can even fire a round or two from my six-gun. You can make it look like a fair fight if you want to."

"Pick it up," said Nate.

"No," said Ira.

Nate slipped the revolver from his holster and pointed it at Ira's gut. "Pick it up, I said."

Ira stood silent.

"Damn it, Ira. Pick up the gun."

Still, Ira stood motionless and silent, and Nate pulled the trigger, sending a bullet into the dirt just by Ira's left foot. Ira didn't flinch. "Pick it up," Nate shouted. Ira didn't move. Nate fired another shot, the bullet coming dangerously close to Ira's left ear. Ira still did not reach down for the gun at his feet. Nate felt a moment of panic. In spite of his threats, he did not want to shoot Ira in cold blood. He wanted a fight. He wanted to best him in a duel. He had not counted on this. He didn't know what to do. A thought flashed through his mind that maybe Ira was waiting for him to empty his revolver, and then he would kill him. But he dismissed that thought. How would Ira know that Nate wouldn't shoot him down? Then he had another thought.

"All right, you son of a bitch," he said. "Don't fight me. I'm going to find your pretty little wife, and I'm going to tell her the whole story. I'm going to tell her your real name, and I'm going to tell her how you and me used to run whores and rob banks and such. And then I'm going to tell her what I done for you and how you turned on me. I'm going to let her know just what a cowardly bastard you really are."

He holstered his revolver and walked over to his horse. As he put his foot in the stirrup to mount up, Ira flung himself through the air, grabbing Nate, and both men fell hard to the ground and rolled in the dirt. "You stay away from her," Ira shouted, pounding a fist into the side of Nate's head.

"Ha," Nate said through clenched teeth. "I got to you, did I?" He beat at Ira's ribs with both his fists.

Ira tried to pin Nate's arms down with his own arms, and in the attempt, he felt the Webley in Nate's jacket pocket. He managed to get his hand in the pocket and pull out the gun. He cocked it and placed the barrel against Nate's temple. "Hold it," he said.

Nate quit struggling, and Ira slowly backed off him and stood up. Carefully, he reached down with his left hand and pulled the revolver out of Nate's holster. Still pointing the Webley at Nate, he moved back to where he had left his own gun and belt on the ground, and he picked them up. "Okay," he said. "Now you can mount up."

Nate climbed into the saddle, all the while looking warily at the gun in Ira's hand. "Where we going?" he asked.

Ira mounted up, still pointing the gun barrel at Nate. "We're going just where you said you were going. We're going to my house to see my wife, but we're going on my terms, not yours. Get moving."

Again they rode in silence, and by the time they reached the Thomas home, it was still midafternoon. As far as Mrs. Thomas knew, her husband was still at the store. About a hundred yards from the house, Nate reined in.

"Keep going," said Ira.

"What are we doing here?" Nate asked. "I said I was going to tell on you. You want me to do that?"

"No," Ira said. "I'm going to tell Kate the whole story. I'm going to tell her myself. Then I'm going to tell her that you came here to kill me, and I'm going to tell her that I won't shoot it out with you. If you want to kill me, you'll just have to do it in cold blood. Once I've told her, I'll give you back your guns."

"That's crazy," Nate said. "What's that going to get you?"

"Nothing," said Ira, "but she'll know. When I'm dead, she'll know why. She'll know the truth, and at least for a little while before I die, I won't be living a lie with her anymore. Now, get moving."

They rode on up to the house. Kate heard their approach and came out on the porch to see who was riding up. "Richard," she said, "what are you doing home at this hour?" She saw the gun in his hand, and her face registered fear and worry.

"Oh," said Ira. He stuck the Webley in his pocket. "It's all right. I brought an old friend to meet you, and I have something to tell you."

Kate shot a worried look at Nate, then turned back toward her husband. "What is it?" she said.

"Not much," said Nate, speaking up quickly. "Me and your husband—Richard—we used to be good friends. We punched cows together for a few years. Why, we was the best of friends, me and ole Richard here. That's why I wouldn't give you my name this morning in your store. You see, we hadn't seen each other for over seven years, and I wanted to surprise him. That's all."

"Oh," she said. "Well, will you be coming in to supper with us? It will be a little while yet. I didn't expect Richard home until after five." Her voice betrayed lingering suspicion. The story Nate had told would have seemed all right, but there was the gun that Richard had been holding when the two men first rode up.

"No, ma'am," Nate said. "Thank you just the same. You see, I have to be moving on. That's the reason Richard closed up the store early. It's the only way we'd have had any time to visit. I'm leaving town right away. I have pressing business elsewhere."

He tipped his hat, turned his mount, and started riding back toward Tombstone. He waited for a word from Ira to stop him. He waited for a gunshot that would send hot lead tearing into his back. There was nothing. He rode on a few yards, then stopped the horse. Twisting in the saddle, he looked back at the Thomases. He raised the hat off his head and waved it. "So long, Richard," he shouted. "Ma'am, it was a pleasure meeting you."

Then he kicked the horse into a gallop and headed for town. He wondered if a stagecoach would be leaving yet before dark. If not, for sure there would be one out of town in the morning. He would be on it, no matter where it was headed.

SPEECHES DELIVERED BY
ROBERT J. CONLEY

Commencement Speech

I am happy to be here with you today on this occasion. I am particularly pleased and proud that my first commencement address—my first invitation to serve at a graduation—came from an Indian college.

Graduation, at any level, is a significant event in any life. Graduation is for *us*, for American Indian people, I believe, even more significant, more meaningful, than it is for most others.

In 1932, only eight years before I was born, according to the BIA Education Division, there were only 385 Indians enrolled in college nationwide, and there were only 52 known Indian college graduates. In 1952, when I was twelve years old, there were only about 100,000 Indian children enrolled in any school at any level. The Navajo tribe alone has a larger population than that. In the late 1950s, of the Indians who started high school, 60 percent did not finish. In 1966, it was widely known and accepted that most Indians did not go to college, and of those who did, 50 percent did not even intend to finish, and an even higher percentage did, in fact, drop out.

These figures are improving, but higher education is still a very recent pursuit for Native American people. It's still new to us. And because of that, our accomplishments in that area are all the more meaningful to us.

You graduates here today are helping to answer two big questions with your achievements. The first question is, Can Indians be successful in contemporary society? You know, when Captain Richard Henry Pratt decided to set up the first boarding school for Indians, the school that became Carlisle Indian School and the first federal Indian school in the history of the United States, he had to first convince white Americans and the United States government that Indians were educable—that Indians were capable of being educated. Now, over one hundred years later, we shouldn't have to keep answering that same old question—but we do. We still have to convince some non-Indians. But worse—we have to continue to convince ourselves. Many Indian people, because of things that have happened to them in their lives, do not believe that they are intelligent. Not so many years ago, rural Oklahoma public schools, without a single test, automatically placed Indian first grade children in a slow learners' class. It takes many years for a child to overcome that experience. Some never do. They become convinced that what everyone is telling them is true—that they are not capable of being educated.

Each one of you graduating here today has made an important and positive step for all American Indian people. Of course Indians are educable. Yes, we can do it. Certainly, you are capable of accomplishing anything that any other human being is capable of accomplishing.

Another question that's been asked time and again is, Are Indian people or Indian tribes capable of running their own schools? The Cherokee Nation, before Oklahoma statehood, ran its own school system. It was the first free compulsory public education system in North America—possibly in the world. It was the prototype of the modern American public education system, and it included the first institution of higher education west of the Mississippi River. By 1907 (the year of Oklahoma statehood), the tiny Cherokee Nation had produced more college graduates than the states of Arkansas and Texas combined. With statehood, the new state of Oklahoma took the school system away from the Cherokees, and after seventy years of state control of Cherokee education, the average adult Cherokee in eastern Oklahoma, according to 1970 census figures, had only five and a half years of school. The Cherokee experience proved years ago that Indians are better at educating Indians than anyone else. Yet that lesson, if it was ever really learned, has been forgotten, so we are having to prove it all over again. This ceremony for Nebraska Indian Community College helps to prove that fact once again. It helps to answer that question. Yes, Indians can run their own education systems. In fact, they can do a better job of it than can anyone else.

These are issues that mean a great deal to me, and I'm proud to be here today. As an American Indian, I'm proud of the Winnebago, Omaha, and Santee Sioux tribes for Nebraska Indian Community

College, and I'm proud of you graduates for what you've achieved. Your tribes should be proud of you. Your friends and your families all have a right to be proud of you. And what's more, you have a right, a personal right which you have earned, to take pride in your own accomplishments. Congratulations to you all. Thank you for inviting me to take part in this important day, and thank you for your attention.

Awards Ceremony

I don't often make speeches for occasions. I'm not often asked to speak, unless it's about my own work or about the profession of writing. But when Mr. Finch called and asked me if I would say a few words for this occasion today, I said that I would be pleased to do so.

You know, we constantly see our student athletes honored for their accomplishments. We read about them in the newspapers every day. We even see them on the evening news on television. I'm not opposed to that. I'm not anti-sports, but I do often think that our sense of what is important in contemporary life is somewhat out of joint.

Our major celebrities are movie stars, television stars, rock musicians, and sports figures. During times of international crises, generals join their ranks. And then, of course, there are the politicians.

But think back a few generations, and even farther. The stars of the past have largely been forgotten. I watched a television interview with Rod Steiger, an Academy Award–winning actor, who told about a time when he had not made a movie for several years. He was ready to get back to work, and he had gotten himself an appointment with a studio executive. He found out in the executive's office that the man did not even know who he was.

Who were the stars during the lifetime of Hemingway and Steinbeck, of Mark Twain—of Shakespeare—of Sophocles? We don't remember them, but we do remember the writers. Or—what's more important—we remember their work. And there's a reason for that. The writers are the chroniclers of their times. They're the conscience of their times. Writers understand and explain their times as no one else does and as no one else can do.

For those reasons and more, we need to consciously cultivate writers. And this is one way to do that, to write. And I, for one, am especially pleased when time is set aside to recognize the accomplishments of young writers. We need, in ceremonies such as this, to show our appreciation for work well done and for the effort to produce good work.

Perhaps even more important, we need to show our students, our young people, that *we* care about good writing. When a student writes a good story, a good poem, a good essay, we need to show that young person and others that we are proud of that accomplishment, we respect it, and we recognize as fact that that accomplishment in writing is, in the long run, just as important as—no, more important than—a touchdown.

For that reason, for all of those reasons, I'm pleased to be here. I'm honored to be here, and I even feel an obligation to be here today—to say how glad I am that this is happening here in the library, and to say to all the students who participated in this event, good for you. Keep it up. And I'm pleased to offer my personal hearty and sincere congratulations to all the winners. What you're doing is important and necessary. And finally, I'm pleased to express my appreciation to all of you for allowing me the privilege of being here to participate in this awards program.

Acceptance Speech

Thank you to all the judges and members of the Oklahoma Center for the Book for this very prestigious award. By the way, I've always wanted to know just what book that is. Can anyone here tell me?

It's always great to receive any award. It's a recognition of all the work we writers do, and often we don't get all that much recognition. A writer works alone, and even when he gets an audience, he is separated from that audience, so the recognition is most welcome. It is, if nothing else, acknowledgment that the work has at least been noticed by someone. And it's especially good to receive such an award from one's home state. I feel good right now being in Oklahoma to receive this honor.

It's especially gratifying to be placed in the company of such great writers as the previous winners of this award: Daniel Boorstin, Tony Hillerman, Savoie Lottinville, Harold Keith, N. Scott Momaday, R. A. Lafferty, John Hope Franklin, S. E. Hinton, Jack Bickham, Michael Wallis, Bill Wallace, Joyce Carol Thomas, Joy Harjo, Carolyn Hart, C. J. Cherryh, Bob Burke, Clifton Taulbert, and David Dary. David, by the way, is not an Oklahoman. He moved here from Kansas and had the good sense and taste to stay.

Oklahoma has produced a great many fine writers in addition to those I just named: in no particular order, but just off the top of my head, Will Rogers, Angie Debo, Rennard Strickland, Jack and Anna Kilpatrick, John Milton Oskison, John Joseph Mathews, Lynn Riggs, Grant Foreman, Emmet Starr, D. L. Birchfield, C. B. Clark, Jerald C. Walker, Rilla Askew, Stan Hoig, Fred Harris, and Teresa Miller. I know that I've left out a great many, and I apologize to each one of them for that. I'm always a little leery about popping off such a list because I know that I'll feel guilty later because of those I forgot to mention. I should add, though, that a number of these writers are right here in the room with us, and that's gratifying. And isn't it wonderful and fitting that we have an organization in the state that exists to promote Oklahoma authors, celebrate the state's literary heritage, and encourage reading for pleasure by Oklahomans? I can't keep myself from mentioning the fact that a fair number of the writers I've named here tonight are Native American, and I've believed for several years that Native American writers are among the nation's best. Alexander Solzhenitsyn, who is not Native American, said that "literature is the living memory of a nation," and Native Americans have long national memories to draw on and to add to. But I should get back to Oklahoma. I'm living in North Carolina now, and I love it. It's the original Cherokee country, and it's a great place to be. But I'm an Oklahoman, and I'll be an Oklahoman till the day I die. I was born in Cushing. My father sold oil field supplies for a living. I was forcibly removed to Texas at an early age, and I resented it, and I've never quite gotten over it. I'm an Okie.

I was forced to relocate to different states in my life in order to have a job and a paycheck, and from time to time I would travel to conferences, where someone would give me a nametag to wear. Under my name would be the state I had come from—for instance, Iowa. Someone would meet me, look at the nametag, and say, "So you're from Iowa." I would say, "No, I'm working in Iowa just now, but I'm from Oklahoma."

Oklahoma is in my blood. Most of what I write is written about Oklahoma. I talk, I think, like Oklahoma. I dress Oklahoma. I love Oklahoma. Having said that, I'll quickly add that there are things about Oklahoma's past and about its present that I do not like. I don't like the way Oklahoma was wrenched from the hands of the Indian tribes here to bring about statehood. I don't like toll roads. I don't like the pride that some Okies take in the name "Sooners," and I don't like the fact that the huge football field used to cast its giant shadow over the tiny university press building. I do like the fact that the press has now moved off the main campus and away from that football field, but they still call the team "Sooners."

I assume that everyone here knows what a sooner is, but just in case anyone does not know, I'll tell you. I jump on any chance to talk about this. When the Boomers lined up in Kansas, ready for the great land rush that would take all that Indian land away, there were some dirty little sneaky thieves who refused to wait and play the game according to the rules. These conniving, greedy cheats sneaked across the line early to mark their claims, and they were the SOONERS. Why are we proud of them? When I say I'm an Okie, I'm not claiming any heritage from the sooners.

When I first met Simon Ortiz, the renowned Acoma poet, he looked at me and said, "You're not anything like what I expected you to be, *Professor* Conley. Hell, you're just a damn Okie." I liked that. It made me feel good.

There's still much to be written about Oklahoma, and I intend to do some of the writing. Two different people have told me already that receiving a lifetime achievement award does not mean that I'm finished and ready for the grave. And I do have other things to write about. I'd like to write a book about Tom Starr, maybe even one about Belle Starr, although she's not one of my favorite characters. Maybe I'll just write a family epic about the whole Starr bunch. I might even want to write about Stand Watie, not the most admirable figure I know about but certainly a very colorful one. I have already written about Henry Starr, a novel and an essay. In my essay I wrote that I admire Henry Starr for having robbed more banks than any man in history, and I meant that. I would love to be a bank robber if the times and high technology hadn't stacked the deck against them.

My favorite people in the world are all artists: writers, painters, sculptors, musicians, actors, dancers, bank robbers, boxers, and all artists. Perhaps the writer is the most fortunate of the bunch, for he can write himself into any or all of these characters. He can be a painter, a sculptor, a musician, an actor, a dancer, a bank robber, a bull rider, or a boxer. I have not yet been a musician or a dancer, but I have been all the others, and it was all great fun. And I suspect that's the best thing about being a writer. It's just all the damn good fun. I hope I haven't bored any of you here tonight. I thank all of you for hanging with me through it all, and once again, I thank the Oklahoma Center for the Book for a wonderful and a great evening. Thank you all.

A Reevaluation of Sequoyah's Final Trip

I have written elsewhere that Sequoyah is at once the best-known and the least-known Cherokee. His birth year is given by different writers with as much as a twenty-year discrepancy.[1] His death date is disputed, and his final resting place has been identified "positively" in at least five different places. He is said to have had from one to five wives and from two to twenty children. There are other mysteries about his life and work. But what I want to examine here are the reasons for his last trip, that mysterious trip to Mexico. In order to do that, I have to go back to the old Cherokee country and the year 1818. Sam Houston had been assigned by President Andrew Jackson to do what he could to persuade Cherokees to move to Arkansas. Houston had persuaded John Jolly and some three hundred more Cherokees to do so. One of those who had signed up for emigration was Sequoyah.[2] Cherokees who favored emigration were threatened with death, and Sequoyah had his name removed from the list. I expect that he felt as if he had just escaped death. He did, however, go ahead and move to Arkansas with his family in 1824.[3]

In 1827, Sequoyah, Black Fox, Thomas Graves, Thomas Maw, George Marvis, John Looney, and John and James Rogers were sent to Washington as a delegation from the Western Cherokee Nation in Arkansas. They were to arrange for a survey of their Arkansas lands, see about overdue annuities, and "do and perform any and everything which they in their best judgement shall deem most likely to conduce to the interest and happiness of the people of their nation."[4] Unbeknownst to the Cherokees, the government had already decided to move the Western Cherokees from their homes, and they began to insist on a land exchange, the Arkansas land for the land of Lovely's Purchase in what is now northeast Oklahoma. The Cherokee delegation resisted, not having the authority from their government to exchange lands. They had, in fact, been instructed to not give up any land.

The U.S. was insistent, though, and practically held the Cherokee delegation captive. The Cherokees had arrived in Washington on February 8th, and by the end of April, they gave in. They signed the treaty agreeing to give up the land in Arkansas and move to Lovely's Purchase.[5] When at last they returned to their homes in western Arkansas, they found poles set in the yards in front of their homes. When they asked what the poles were for, they were told, "to set your heads on." James Spear "struck [James] Rogers in the head twice with a large rock. And as Rogers left the agency, Chief White Path hurled rocks at him and threatened to kill him." A council meeting was scheduled "to try the delegation for betrayal of their trust," though somehow the threats were not carried out.[6] The Cherokee Nation made the move to Lovely's Purchase in 1829. Once again, Sequoyah had squeaked by with his life.

Then in 1839, Sequoyah joined with 250 other Western Cherokees to depose Western Chiefs Brown and Rogers because they would not take part in a council designed to join all the Cherokees back together again under one government. On September 6, 1839, they met in Tahlequah and formed a government under Principal Chief John Ross, abolishing the Western Cherokee Nation.[7] Not surprisingly, many of the Western Cherokees were angered by this action. Sequoyah must have felt that he was pushing his luck. This made three times he had angered his tribesmen.

In the spring of 1842, he decided to make a trip to Mexico. He recruited his son Teesee, a man known as the Worm, and six other young Cherokees. He admonished the Worm not to tell anyone where they were going. He did not allow them the leisure to hunt until they had crossed the Red River. The story of Sequoyah's trip to Mexico is well documented, having been told later by the Worm, and it is not necessary to retell it here. He made it to Mexico, where he found the Cherokees who had gone there earlier, and he died among them, probably in 1843. The location of his burial has not been discovered.

Sequoyah had placed his life in danger on three separate occasions, and that is not counting the years he was engaged in perfecting the syllabary. During that time he was accused of witchcraft, ridiculed, and scorned by many. The other three occasions were more specific. He had signed up to move to Arkansas at a time when just expressing favorable views regarding that move could be fatal. He had nearly gotten himself killed over the treaty that he and the other delegates had signed in Washington. And finally, he had deposed the Western Chiefs and abolished their government. I believe that with his trip to Mexico, Sequoyah was running for his life.

NOTES

1. In 1828 while in Washington, Sequoyah told Samuel Knapp that he was about sixty-five, placing his birth date at around 1763. Cherokee historian Grant Foreman supports a date of 1773 or later. In 1835 John Howard Payne was read a biography of Sequoyah by George Lowery and was told that Sequoyah was about sixty at that time, placing his birth around 1775. Stan Hoig believes it is likely that Sequoyah was born in 1778. See Samuel L. Knapp, account of meeting with Sequoyah in "Lecture I," in *Lectures on American Literature, with Remarks on Some Passages of American History* (New York: Elam Bliss, 1829), 25–29, also reprinted as "See-Quah-Yah, the Cherokee Philosopher," *Cherokee Phoenix* 2, no. 17 (July 29, 1829): 1–2; Grant Foreman, *Sequoyah* (Norman: University of Oklahoma Press, 1938), 77; Stan Hoig, *Sequoyah: The Cherokee Genius* (Oklahoma City: Oklahoma Historical Society, 1995), 107–8.

2. Hoig, *Sequoyah*, 25.

3. Sequoyah (listed as George Guess) was actually one of 837 "emigrants" who changed their minds in a memorial and refused to leave. Other prominent Cherokees who signed agreements to move west and changed their minds included Yonaguska, who became the leader of the "Eastern Band of Cherokees"; Junaluska, hero of the Creek War; Spring Frog, an early Western Cherokee leader who was a "naturalist and sportsman of note"; and Bushyhead, a name prominent in both the Cherokee Nation of Oklahoma and the Eastern Band of Cherokee Indians. For the complete list, see National Archives, RG 75, Records of the Cherokee Indian Agency in Tennessee, 1801–1835, M208, reel 8.

4. Hoig, *Sequoyah*, 59. Hoig points out that the Treaty of 1828 was remarkably similar to the Treaty of New Echota in 1835. Both were sham treaties that the U.S. government conducted with a small group of Cherokees who were not empowered to make such a treaty. Not only had the Cherokee delegation greatly exceeded their power, but many, if not all, received bribes. Thomas Graves received $1,200; Sequoyah received $500 and rights to a saline in Lee's Creek; while James Rogers also received $500. Stan Hoig, *The Cherokees and Their Chiefs: In the Wake of Empire* (Fayetteville: University of Arkansas Press, 1998), 139.

5. For a brief history of Lovely's Purchase, made by William Lovely, see Charles C. Royce, *The Cherokee Nation of Indians* (Chicago: Aldine, 1975), 117–21.

6. Hoig, *Sequoyah*, 65.

7. Grace Steele Woodward, *The Cherokees* (Norman: University of Oklahoma Press, 1963), 228.